Strawberries and Strangers – Pelican Cove Cozy Mystery Series Book 1

By Leena Clover

First Published – May 1, 2018

Leena Clover

Acknowledgements

This book would not have been possible without the loving support of several people. Many thanks to my friend and mentor Bob who is a constant source of inspiration and advice. Thank you to my sibling who questions every plot point and much more to make the story better. Thank you to my beta readers and advanced readers who provide valuable feedback in the nick of time. Thanks to all my readers who motivate me to keep writing. Above all, thanks to my family who provide a support system that enables me to write the stories in my head.

I truly appreciate your assistance.

Strawberries and Strangers

For A

Chapter 1

Jenny King breathed in the cool salty breeze rolling off the Atlantic. She shivered a bit in her light cardigan as a smile lit up her face. The sun had risen over the ocean a couple of hours ago and the sunny spring day already looked promising. It was a big day for her.

She rubbed the tiny gold four-leaf clover that hung around her neck on a chain. It gave her immense strength and was the only tangible connection she had to her son Nick. Nick, now a college freshman, had started giving her a charm as a Mother's Day gift ever since he turned eight. All the charms had dangled around her wrist on a bracelet for years. She had strung them on a chain earlier that year. They literally touched her heart and comforted her in a time of turmoil.

"More coffee?" she asked her favorite customer.

"Stop fawning over me, sweetie, and skedaddle. You have bigger fish to fry today."

"We're all set, Auntie, don't worry."

"What did I tell you about that?" the brightly dressed woman with eyes as green as the sea complained. "You make me sound old."

At 66, Rebecca King was no

spring chicken but she insisted her niece call her Star like everyone else.

"Are you invited?"

"I have a standing invitation to this shindig," Rebecca King alias Star preened. "I married a Cox, didn't I?"

"And the Coxes and the Newburys are tight. Is that it, Star?"

"I wouldn't say that, Jenny."

"I'm still getting it right in my head," Jenny admitted.

"You know I don't give a damn about all this snobbery."

"You're the most down to earth

person I know," Jenny nodded, giving her aunt a quick hug.

Jenny had arrived in the small seaside town of Pelican Cove three months ago. She had been in shock. She realized that now. Who wouldn't be? Her marriage of twenty years had just come to an abrupt end. Her husband William Anderson had coolly come home with a young svelte woman in tow and announced his plans. The young woman was expecting his child and what choice did he have but to marry her? He demanded a divorce and told Jennifer to clear out.

Jenny had some rights but her husband was a hotshot lawyer. He tied up all their assets and promised her she would get nothing if she made a fuss. Too outraged to argue, Jenny had meekly fallen in line with whatever William said.

Jenny had wanted to get as far away from her suburban mansion as possible. Her Aunt Becca or Star had come to the rescue. Star was the oddball in the family, living on a little known island somewhere off the coast of Virginia. She had hitchhiked her way across the country in the 1970s and come upon this small town she called her own piece of paradise. The salt marshes and ocean had captured her heart and Star had stayed on. The scenic village offered the perfect inspiration for her art. Then she fell in love with a local. Pelican Cove became her home. She had called Jennifer and ordered her to come visit.

"You get over here, young lady," Star had thundered on the phone. "We'll put you right in no time."

All Jenny knew about Pelican Cove was that it was quiet and isolated. Nothing much happened there according to her aunt. It sounded like the perfect place to lick her wounds. So Jenny had packed a bag and walked out on her old life. She had been in a daze when she arrived in Pelican Cove. She took long walks on the beach and sat for hours in a small café, staring at the sea. The locals had welcomed her warmly and let her be. One day Star suggested she work part time at the café just to keep busy.

"I've never worked in a café!" she had protested.

"You can start now," Star quipped. "Or you can take up a paintbrush and start painting seascapes alongside me."

"You like to cook, don't you?" Petunia Clark, the lady who owned the café had asked.

Petunia was about Star's age, and her best friend on the island.

"Your aunt says you threw a lot of parties for your husband?"

"I'm used to entertaining," Jenny admitted grudgingly. "And I do love to cook. It's pretty much what I did all my life."

"Well then," Petunia had bobbed her head up and down, making her two chins wobble. "You can start by pouring coffee."

Three months later, Jenny King was a fixture at the café. She did much more than pour coffee. Petunia had discovered how good a cook Jenny was early on. She had revamped the café menu and encouraged Jenny to put her skills to use. Jenny loved using the abundant local produce and fresh seafood. The locals were reluctant at first but they soon fell in love with her peculiar brand of cooking. Jenny baked and cooked like there was no tomorrow. She loved being exhausted at the end of the day. That meant she was out like a light the moment her head hit the pillow. Jenny didn't want to spare a thought for her sorry past.

Jenny felt a hand on her back and turned to smile at Petunia.

"All set for the party?" the older woman asked kindly. "This is all thanks to you, Jenny. Ada Newbury never set a foot in this café before you got here."

Jenny blushed but said nothing.

The Newburys were the richest family in the town of Pelican

Cove. Although they didn't share the honor of being the 'first family', they tried to make up for it with plenty of wealth. Rumor had it their coffers were full of gold, gold they had dug up from the sea. They had a sprawling ocean facing estate spread over ten acres. Unlike most houses in town, it was newly built. Anything built in the last fifty years was considered new in Pelican Cove.

"But you've been open twenty five years, haven't you, Petunia?"

"That's just how long I owned this café, dear. It was around a long time before that."

"So the Newburys never came to the Boardwalk Café?"

"They got rich in the great storm," Petunia whispered, leaning forward. "And they built that big castle of theirs."

"Upstarts!" Star snorted.

Petunia rolled her eyes and turned toward Jenny.

"They got rich and uppity, I tell you. I guess they thought coming to this café was beneath them."

"Then why have they hired us now?" Jenny asked.

"It's all because of you," Petunia sang. "That and the fancy caterer they hired from the mainland cancelled at the last minute."

"I'm no match for a caterer,"

Jenny said humbly.

"Betty Sue Morse can't stop singing your praises," Star explained. "She goes on and on about your strawberry cheesecake and the cupcakes you bake for the inn. When Ada raised a fuss about having no one to cater their Spring Gala, Betty Sue told her she couldn't do better than you."

Betty Sue Morse was Pelican Cove and Pelican Cove couldn't exist without Betty Sue Morse. She was the fourth descendant of James Morse, the original owner of Pelican Cove. It had been called Morse Isle at the time.

James Morse of New England travelled south with his wife

Caroline and his three children in 1837. He bought the island for $125 and named it Morse Isle. He built a house for his family on a large tract of land. Fishing provided him with a livelihood, so did floating wrecks. He sent for a friend or two from up north. They came and settled on the island with their families. They in turn invited their friends. Morse Isle soon became a thriving community.

Being a barrier island, it took a battering in the great storm of 1962. Half the island was submerged forever. Most of that land had belonged to the Morse family. A new town emerged in the aftermath of the storm and it was named Pelican Cove.

Jenny shook her head as she thought of the town's colorful history. She hadn't had an inkling of all that when she came there a few months ago. Now she was fascinated by the history of the island and the stories of the families that had settled there over the years.

"Does anyone say no to Betty Sue?" Jenny mused.

"Why should they?" Star argued. "She's right most of the time. And she's a Morse."

"Being a Morse is a big deal here, isn't it?" Jenny asked, fascinated.

Star and Petunia both nodded emphatically.

"Is that why she didn't change her name?" Jenny asked.

"Betty Sue said she was born a Morse and she would die a Morse. That was her condition when she got married."

"And her kids would have the name Morse too," Petunia added with relish. "That's what she named her son."

"So that's why Heather's a Morse," Jenny said, referring to Betty Sue's granddaughter and her new friend.

"Heather's the last Morse alive," Petunia added. "She better find a man soon and get cracking."

"So the Morses and Newburys are

Pioneers?" Jenny asked. "Who else?"

Jenny still couldn't wrap her head around the different local families. She found the dynamics fascinating.

"Cotton, Stone and Williams..." Star chanted. "There are five Pioneer families. Then there are the Survivors."

"That's your husband's family, right?" Jenny asked her aunt.

"The Coxes came off the Bella alright," Star nodded. "Swam their way to the island."

She was referring to the survivors of an old shipwreck. The summer of 1876 had brought tragedy to the island. A passing steamship, the Isabella, had sunk in the shoals. Plenty of people had gone down with her. There were only seventeen survivors who were rescued and brought to Morse Isle. They stayed on and never went back. Their families thrived on in Pelican Cove, still referred to as the Survivors. Star's deceased husband had been one of them.

"That makes you one of them, right Auntie?" Jenny asked. "I mean, Star."

Star threw back her head and laughed.

"Nothing will make me one of them. I may have lived here for over forty years but I'm still a chicken necker. That's a newcomer."

"What about me? I just got here."

"Enough of that, Jenny," Petunia rushed. "You can talk all you want about the island after this party. We need to get going now."

"Aren't you going to change?" Star asked Jenny, roving a critical eye over her stained apron and wrinkled jeans.

"I'm wearing my yellow dress," Jenny nodded.

"Folks are going to love your cheesecake," Petunia said eagerly.

"What about Ada Newbury?"

25

Jenny asked worriedly. "Do you think she'll be pleased?"

"As far as I remember, Ada Newbury has never had a kind word for anyone," Star dismissed. "I wouldn't take it to heart if I were you."

"I'm sure the people of Pelican Cove will love your cake," Petunia told Jenny loyally. "And they'll be flocking to the Boardwalk Café to get more of it."

"How many people turn up for this gala?" Jenny asked.

"About a hundred people are invited to the buffet," Petunia explained. "These are the top local families and guests from out of town."

"What about the picnickers?" Star asked. "There could be hundreds more."

Petunia pursed her lips in thought.

"This is the one day of the year the Newbury estate is thrown open to the public," she explained to Jenny. "People are allowed to roam free on the beaches. Many of them bring a picnic and spend the day at the beach."

"Do they have live music?" Jenny asked eagerly.

"Nothing of the sort," Star grumbled. "But don't worry. There are a few people I want you to meet."

"You're not…" Jenny frowned. "You promised!"

"Life goes on, Jenny. You need to pick yourself up and start having some fun."

"I'm not ready yet," Jenny told her firmly.

"You will be when you meet this guy."

Chapter 2

Jenny hitched a ride to the party with her aunt. Star was wearing a tie dyed kaftan with every color of the rainbow in it. Jenny had changed into her yellow sun dress but she wore a sweater over it just in case.

"Petunia's gone ahead to make sure everything is set up correctly," she told Star.

"You've done your bit, girl," Star told her. "Now just let your hair down and enjoy yourself."

"I hardly know anyone there," Jenny said, feeling anxious all of a sudden.

"You know enough people."

"Will Heather be there?" Jenny asked.

"Heather will be there with Chris," Star counted off. "Old Eddie Cotton is closing the pub to come to the party. Pa Williams will be there too."

Heather Morse was a shy young woman Jenny had taken to immediately. Heather ran the Bayview Inn along with her grandma Betty Sue. Chris Williams was her beau. They both came from the much esteemed Pioneer families of Pelican Cove.

"What about Molly?" Jenny asked, thinking of her other friend.

Molly Henderson was the local

librarian. She was Heather's age, a decade younger than Jenny but they both shared a love for the local seafood. Jenny had struck up a quick friendship with the smart and energetic 33 year old.

"I'm afraid Molly doesn't make the cut," Star said, making a face.

"Why not?" Jenny bristled. "She's one of the smartest people on the island."

"Only one thing counts with the Newburys," Star said. "Or two. Money and lineage. Molly's got neither."

"I'm not sure I like these people," Jenny said.

She had a sudden flashback to

her husband's friends. They could give these Newburys a few lessons in snobbery. She was glad she was rid of them. She shook off the thought, resolving to enjoy the day.

"Give them a chance," Star shrugged.

The car climbed uphill for a bit and came abreast some massive iron gates. The guard waved them through. He was a local and he knew Star very well.

Lush green lawns spread as far as the eye could see. The ocean pounded the shore in the distance. Jenny could see groups of people strolling along the beach. A game of volleyball was in progress. Some people had set up camp chairs and were sipping drinks from coolers. Others relaxed on blankets, eating out of straw baskets.

"This is so festive," she exclaimed.

"You're not going there," Star said, inching her car along the driveway.

She pointed toward a sprawling mansion that loomed over them.

"That's where you're going, missy."

Star handed her car over to a valet. He turned out to be another young kid from town. He whispered something in Star's ear and she smiled.

"Is there anyone you don't know, Star?" Jenny said, suddenly feeling like an outsider.

"I used to babysit him," Star said lightly. "When you live here for forty some years, you can't help knowing people."

Jenny wondered if she would be alive in forty years. At 44, she figured the chances were slim to none. She fiddled with one of the charms on her necklace, flexed her shoulders and stood up straight.

"Let's go," she nodded, putting her game face on.

She was trying hard to ignore the

butterflies in her stomach.

Ada Newbury stood in the cavernous foyer, greeting her guests. She barely spared a glance for Star.

"Hello Ada," Star said, thrusting herself in her host's face. "Have you met my niece?"

"Jenny King," Jenny said cheerfully, offering her hand.

Ada ignored it and tipped her head.

"Petunia's setting up in the back. I am sure she needs your help."

"Jenny's been baking her butt off for you," Star scowled. "She's here as your guest."

A tall man with a receding hairline and grey hair at the temples burst in on them. He was well rounded across the middle. He wore a benevolent look unlike the woman he sidled next to. He put an arm around her shoulder and greeted Star with a smile.

"Well, well, it's our very own artist," he boomed. "When are you painting the view from our north tower, Star?"

"Whenever Ada gives me the keys to the tower," Star laughed, grasping the man's hand. "How are you, Julius?"

"Never been better," Julius said with a smile. "And who's this pretty young lady next to you?"

Introductions were made and the man turned out to be Ada's husband. He was her complete opposite. Jenny realized he was the one with the actual bloodline Ada was so snobbish about. She wondered where Ada had come from. Was she even an islander?

"The marquee's set up in the rose garden," Julius Newbury told Star. "Ya'll have a good time now."

Star dragged Jenny along with her without sparing another glance for their hostess. Jenny ogled the Persian rugs and giant art lining the walls as she made her way behind her aunt. The Newburys were certainly not hurting for money. They burst onto a patio full of people. Long rows of rose bushes extended as far as the eye could see. Waves lapped against the shore in the distance. A big marquee was erected along one side, with tables for food and drinks. Satin covered tables and chairs were strewn around. Small groups of people hung about, eating fancy food off dainty plates.

Jenny spotted Petunia near the marquee and walked over.

"What can I help you with?" she asked.

Petunia turned around mid-sentence. She had been busy directing the staff. Her frown turned into a smile.

"The food's flying off the trays, Jenny!" she exclaimed. "People are full of praise. They can't wait to meet you."

Jenny tucked her hair behind her ear, trying to hide a blush.

"It's nothing, really. Can I help hand stuff out?"

"You'll do nothing of that sort," Petunia huffed. "We've hired plenty of staff for that. You just mingle and make friends. I'll take you around myself in a minute."

Star walked into them, eating a large slice of cheesecake. She closed her eyes and moaned with pleasure.

"You have outdone yourself,

Jenny. This is so good!"

"So is the crab dip," Petunia told her. "And the hot and sweet chicken wings and the coconut crusted shrimp."

"Mmmmm..." Star mumbled. "You know I have a big sweet tooth. I went for the desserts first."

"Grab a plate and start eating," Petunia ordered Jenny. "You've been rushed off your feet since 6 AM."

"I am sort of hungry," Jenny admitted.

She started filling a plate with a little of everything. Unlike her aunt, she went for the savories first.

"Jenny!" a voice squealed in her ear and she turned around to hug Heather Morse. "This food is delicious. Grandma can't stop bragging about you."

The brown haired six foot man next to Heather smiled indulgently.

"You're famous, Jenny," he said mildly.

Betty Sue Morse joined the group, looking important. Her petite five foot frame belied her larger than life personality. She looked odd without the ever present knitting in her hand.

"Jenny," she roared, holding her arms wide.

Betty Sue and some of the islanders spoke in a slightly different accent. It was a way of telling the old islanders apart from the newcomers.

Jenny set her plate aside and hugged the delicate seventy five year old woman. Betty Sue was the uncrowned monarch of the island and she didn't let anyone forget that.

"This is the best party Ada has thrown in years. She owes you one."

"So you liked the food, Miss Morse?" Jenny mumbled.

"Like it? People can't stop licking their fingers. Eddie Cotton wants to sell your wings at the Rusty Anchor. I told him to get in line."

"Let the girl eat, Betty Sue," Star grumbled. "She's wilting as you speak."

Star huddled close to Petunia and Betty Sue and the three older women put their heads together.

"What are they up to now?" Jenny asked Heather, chewing delicately on a chicken wing.

It could use a little more pepper, she noted to herself.

"I miss Molly," Heather said. "I told Chris to bring her along."

"Couldn't she drive over herself?" Chris asked.

She flung an accusatory glance at the quiet man.

"Have you forgotten island politics, Chris? No way Ada Newbury is going to invite a refugee into her home."

"I didn't know people still thought that way," Chris admitted. "It seems silly."

"You've been away too long," Heather told him. "Nothing is more important to these people than hierarchy."

"I thought Molly's folks have been in Pelican Cove since the very beginning?" Jenny asked with interest.

"That's right," Heather nodded.

"But Pelican Cove doesn't exist as far as these old timers are concerned. They are still living on Morse Isle."

"Your grandma isn't like that," Jenny mused. "Why is she different?"

"Heather brought her around," Chris beamed. "You can thank her for that."

Heather's cheeks turned pink and she looked away.

A few groups of people had started walking toward the beach. Although part of the same coastline, this beach was some distance away from the other picnickers. A makeshift barrier had been put up cordoning off this section, lest any of the commoners strayed into the elite area.

"Shall we walk along the beach?" Chris asked the ladies.

"Not until I have a piece of Jenny's cheesecake first," Heather said.

She opened her mouth wide and took a big bite of the sinful dessert. It almost stuck in her throat as a piercing scream sounded far away. Heather coughed and sputtered as her food went down the wrong way.

"What was that?" Jenny asked as she patted Heather on the back.

"You girls stay here," Chris ordered. "I'll go have a look."

The old biddies had also heard the scream. They surrounded Jenny and Heather, peppering them with questions.

"Hold on, Grandma," Heather gasped, finally catching her breath. "Chris will be back soon."

Chris came back five minutes later, looking grim. His face was white with shock.

"Bad news!" he declared, raising his hand to ward off their questions. "There's a dead body on the beach. Eddie's grandson almost walked into it."

He gulped as the older ladies

bombarded him with questions.

"I don't know anything else. We'll just to have to wait until someone tells us."

"Look," Betty Sue thundered. "There's Adam. I bet he'll know more than you."

Jenny whipped her head around in the direction of Betty Sue's finger. A man was limping slowly toward the patio. He was taller than Chris and his brown hair was peppered with gray. He held up a hand and let out a piercing whistle.

"It's Adam Hopkins," Heather whispered to Jenny.

Jenny felt a frisson of anticipation as she gazed at the attractive man. She had poured coffee for him plenty of times. She hardly recognized him today, dressed as he was in a fancy suit. Jenny was used to seeing him in his uniform.

People had gathered around Adam. They waited for him to speak, looking around nervously. The news of the dead man had already spread like wildfire through the small crowd. Some people thought it was a prank.

"I have some sad news," Adam began. "We just found the body of a man on the beach. We don't know who he is yet. My folks need to come in and examine the area."

He looked around at the anxious

faces around him.

"I am afraid I can't allow anyone to leave yet. We'll have to take down your names and contact information. We will also need to get a brief statement from all of you."

A buzz passed through the crowd as people started grumbling. The party mood had vanished in an instant.

"You know where I live, Adam," Eddie Cotton was arguing with the man. "I've got to go back and open the Rusty Anchor for business."

"I'm just following procedure, Eddie," the man told him. "You'll have to wait here until we get your statement."

"Can he do that?" Jenny asked Heather.

"Of course he can. Have you forgotten Adam's the Sheriff of Pelican Cove?"

Chapter 3

Jenny stifled a yawn as she poured coffee for her customers the next day. The Boardwalk Café was bursting at the seams. Most of the population of Pelican Cove had turned up for breakfast bright and early, even those who hardly ever came to the café.

"You're going to be very busy today," Star had remarked that morning as Jenny waved goodbye to her. "The vultures will come sniffing."

Petunia looked harried as she arranged a fresh batch of muffins in the display case.

"Can you check the oven please,

Jenny? The next batch should be ready soon."

"I've never seen this place so busy," Jenny remarked as she walked into the kitchen.

"That's because you haven't been here in the summer," Petunia said with a laugh. "You have it easy now, girl. Wait till the tourist season begins."

"You can count on me, Petunia," Jenny said earnestly, putting a hand on the older woman's shoulder. "I'm not afraid of hard work."

"We will hire more help then," Petunia shrugged. "Kids will be out of school and plenty of them will be lining up for a summer job. I would rather use your skills in the kitchen. That's where you make the magic."

Jenny smiled shyly.

"I've never cooked for strangers before, other than the guests my husband brought home."

"Oh honey! That murder upstaged you. Your food would've been the only thing people talked about today if not for that body on the beach."

"Who do you think it is?" Jenny asked curiously, pulling on some mitts before sliding her hand into the hot oven.

She pulled out a pan full of

banana walnut muffins and breathed in the fresh baked aroma.

"These smell yummy," she sighed.

Warm cinnamon and vanilla scented the air around her.

"You need to get off your feet for a few minutes," Petunia clucked. "Why don't you take one of these warm muffins and relax on the deck out back? I'll get you some fresh coffee. I just started a pot."

"What about all the guests?" Jenny protested.

She had the enthusiasm of a new worker and was eager to please.

"They will be fine," Petunia assured her.

Jenny placed a warm muffin on a small plate. Then she scooped up a generous dollop of butter and plopped it on top of the muffin. She carried the plate out to the deck at the back of the café. The section was closed for customers this time of the year. She put her feet up on a chair and bit into her sweet treat. Petunia came along with a tray and two coffee mugs.

"What did you gather from the customers?" she asked Jenny, leaning forward.

Jenny shrugged. She had picked up some gossip even though she hadn't been listening for it.

"No one really knows who that man is. The consensus is that he must be from out of town."

"Of course he is," Petunia grunted, taking a deep sip of her coffee. "Had anyone seen him before the party?"

"Not as far as I know," Jenny said lamely.

She didn't feel comfortable gossiping about a dead man.

"Shouldn't I go out and check on the customers?"

Petunia gave a brief nod.

"Keep an ear out, Jenny. You never know what you might pick up."

A tall, scrawny brown haired woman with thick Coke-bottle eyeglasses rushed into the café, looking over her shoulder.

"Jenny," she called out before she spotted her at the counter. "Oh, you are right here. Got a minute?"

"Sure, Molly. What's up?"

Jenny's face lit up when she saw the harried young woman. Molly was one of the new friends she had made in town.

Molly scurried around the counter and grabbed Jenny by the arm. She almost dragged her into the kitchen.

"It's your aunt. We need to talk."

"Aunt Becca? What's wrong with her?" Jenny asked as her heart skipped a beat.

Star was quite whimsical in her ways. Jenny had found her unpredictable at best. She wondered what new scrape her aunt had got into now.

"I was coming out of the bank, okay?" Molly said in a rush. "The sheriff's car swept past me. I saw your aunt in it."

"Are you sure it was her?" Jenny asked with a smile.

Molly's bad vision was a joke among the friends. She was always peering at people through her glasses, blaming a wrong prescription.

"Your aunt is kind of distinct," Molly huffed. "It was her alright, wearing something colorful."

Jenny thought back to that morning. Star had been wearing yet another tie dyed ensemble.

"What was she doing with the sheriff?" Jenny asked dumbly.

Molly widened her eyes and looked over her shoulder again. She bent down from her six foot high perch and whispered loudly in Jenny's ear.

"I think she was arrested."

"What?" Jenny roared. "Are you out of your mind, Molly?"

"What's all the fuss about, girls?" Petunia asked, coming in with the coffee tray. "Everything alright?"

Jenny was too shocked to answer.

"Star was arrested," Molly declared. "I just saw her in the back of the sheriff's car."

"That's nonsense, Molly," Petunia dismissed. "You must be mistaken. Are you sure you had your glasses on right?"

"There's nothing wrong with my vision," Molly cried out in frustration. "Why don't you try calling home, Jenny? See if your aunt answers."

Jenny had been staying with her aunt since she came to Pelican

Cove. She didn't have her own place yet.

"You know she's never at home this time of the day," Jenny argued. "She probably set up her canvas on the beach somewhere."

Jenny held up her hand as Molly opened her mouth again.

"No. She does not have a cell phone. Doesn't need one, she says."

There was a scurry of footsteps and Betty Sue Morse bustled in, her hands clutching her knitting needles. A ball of bright pink yarn was clutched in her armpit. Her hands worked in tandem and the needles clacked in a rhythm of their own as she tried to catch her breath. Her bosom heaved with the effort.

Heather was at her heels, holding her grandma's black poodle Tootsie in her arms.

"You know you can't bring Tootsie here, Heather," Petunia warned.

"I know, I know. I wanted to make sure Grandma was okay and Toots followed behind. That's why I'm holding her in my arms. I won't let her down, I promise."

Petunia was mollified. She turned to Betty Sue.

"What's got your panties in a wad, Betty Sue?"

Betty Sue looked at Jenny apologetically.

"Star's been arrested. I just saw her going in to the station with the sheriff."

"Are you sure?" Jenny burst out.

Betty Sue puffed up in indignation. No one dared doubt her word in Pelican Cove. She forgot Jenny wasn't aware of her reputation.

Molly stepped in triumphantly.

"Didn't I tell you? Think before you go doubting my eyesight again."

"Wait a minute, wait a minute..." Jenny held up a hand.

"So you people saw Star talking to the sheriff. That's it. That doesn't mean anything."

"Why else would she go to the police station?" Heather asked. "Adam doesn't make small talk."

"You better go, dear," Petunia said, twisting her fingers. "Star might need you to bail her out."

"But I can't abandon you," Jenny protested. "It's our busiest day since I started working here."

She pointed to a group of people who were coming into the café. Another bunch seemed to be loitering on the street, deciding whether to go in or not.

Their conversation hadn't stayed

private. One of the old men pointed his cane at Jenny.

"There's something rotten going on alright. Adam Hopkins doesn't take his job lightly."

Jenny pulled off her apron after Heather promised to help Petunia.

"I'll walk out with you," Molly said with resolve.

Jenny finally felt a sliver of apprehension as she neared the police station. Had her aunt done something wrong? She walked up to the desk and talked to a clerk.

"Star is being questioned," she confirmed Jenny's worst fears. "They just brought her in."

"Has she been arrested?"

"Not yet," the clerk said.

She seemed to know Star very well.

"She's a fine artist. But these artist types are always a bit odd."

"Can someone tell me what's going on?" Jenny demanded. "Does she have a lawyer yet?"

The clerk shrugged and started flipping the pages of a magazine she had under her desk.

Jenny paced the lobby, trying to guess what was going on behind closed doors. There was one door marked Sheriff and another small room beside it. The door to the small room burst open after a while and Adam Hopkins hobbled out. He looked like he hadn't slept in a while. He stood with almost all his weight on his cane. He looked up and stared directly into Jenny's eyes.

"We didn't order anything from the café."

Jenny clucked her tongue.

"Is my aunt here?" she asked urgently.

"Rebecca King?" Adam asked, using Star's full name.

He nodded behind him as Star came out. She smiled when she saw Jenny but she looked a bit flustered. Star opened her arms wide and Jenny flew into them.

"Aunt Becca! What are you doing here? What's wrong?"

"Let's go home," Star said, grabbing Jenny's elbow and pulling her along.

"They haven't arrested you then?" Jenny sighed in relief.

"Not yet," Adam Hopkins drawled. "Remember what I said, Miss King. You can't hide for long."

Star rolled her eyes and started walking out.

"What are you doing here?" Jenny asked as they stepped out in the sun. "Betty Sue and Molly came by the café. They thought you had been arrested."

"I was taken in for questioning," Star said as they walked down Main Street toward the Boardwalk Café.

Jenny couldn't hide her apprehension as they climbed up the steps of the café. She pulled out a chair on the back deck and made her aunt sit.

"Let me get you some coffee."

She barged in and spotted the group of her aunt's friends at a table. They all looked worried. She waved at them and signaled them to come out back.

Star took a sip of the coffee Jenny brought her. Betty Sue, Heather and Petunia sat at the edge of their chairs, waiting for Star to start talking.

"What's going on, Star?" Betty Sue burst out finally. "Why did that Hopkins boy take you to the station?"

"It's about that stranger they found on the beach," Star began. "They found one of my brushes in his pocket."

"Brushes?" Petunia repeated.

"Paintbrush," Star elaborated. "They think I knew the guy."

"Did you?" Jenny asked.

"Of course I didn't," Star said mildly.

"Did you get a good look at him yesterday?" Betty Sue asked.

"Adam showed me a photo," Star said. "I've never set eyes upon that man in my life."

"Then how did he have your paintbrush?" Betty Sue asked.

"That's what Adam wants to know," Star explained. "He thinks I'm lying."

There was a pause as four pairs of eyes stared back at her.

"I'm not!" Star said a bit loudly.

She turned to Jenny.

"I need your help, Jenny. I'm the only suspect the police have so far and I swear I'm innocent."

"I believe you, Auntie," Jenny said, putting a hand on her aunt's shoulder. "But what can I do?"

"You need to find out who did this," Star said primly. "Just like you did last time."

"I just got lucky. I'm not an investigator or anything."

"We'll help you," Betty Sue heaved.

She looked at Petunia and tipped her head.

"Won't we?"

"Of course we will," Petunia bobbed her head. "We look after our own here in Pelican Cove."

Jenny stifled a groan. She didn't know who was more inept at solving a murder, she or her aunt's geriatric friends. Not that she had much of a choice. If her aunt was in trouble, she would have to do something to prove her innocence.

Chapter 4

"Don't you have to get back to the inn?" Jenny asked Heather.

"Breakfast was cleared hours ago," Betty Sue dismissed.

She was knitting furiously, cooing to her poodle at the same time.

"We don't have many guests at this time."

Jenny's eyes widened as she thought of the Bayview Inn. It was one of the first places people came upon when they entered the town of Pelican Cove. Most visitors got a room there.

"Was he one of your guests?" she burst out.

"You think we haven't thought of that?" Heather rolled her eyes. "All our guests are accounted for. Most of them are regulars who take advantage of the offseason discounts. We know them all very well."

"That would have been easy," Betty Sue nodded. "We could have just handed over their information to the sheriff. I never take in a guest without noting down their particulars."

Star was looking peaked. She rubbed her forehead with her fingers.

"Are we making too much of this? Maybe Adam was just doing his job."

"But you are implicated in some way, right?" Jenny asked. "Do we need to get you a lawyer?"

"This is not the big city, Jenny dear. We don't take things that seriously here."

"I think you should," Petunia sniffed. "A man lost his life, Star. That is serious enough."

The three older ladies went back and forth over what needed to be done. Heather cuddled Tootsie, listening to them but saying nothing.

"Are they always like this?" Jenny asked Heather.

Star stood up suddenly and held up a hand.

"Jenny will look into this when she gets a chance. That's good enough for me."

"But I'm working here, Star," Jenny argued. "I don't have time to play detective."

"You're in the perfect spot for this kind of work," Star said. "Just keep your eyes and ears open. Maybe ask a question or two. You're bound to hear something."

"What about that paintbrush?" Jenny asked. "Did you lose one?"

Star shrugged.

"I have dozens of brushes. I am leaving them around all the time."

"Did you tell that to the Sheriff?"

Petunia asked.

"He can find out for himself," Star said with a shrug.

"That brush is the only thing that links you to the crime," Jenny exclaimed in frustration. "Isn't it?"

Her eyes filled with speculation.

"Is that all they have on you?"

"Adam didn't say much," Star conceded.

"That's it. I'm going to go talk to him."

Petunia held her hand out for Jenny's apron. Her eyes had a gleam in them.

"That's right, dear. You go talk to that Adam. Give him a piece of your mind."

Betty Sue suppressed a giggle and Jenny looked hurt.

"Is something funny here?"

"They can't help it," Heather said. "They'll be talking about china patterns the minute you get out of here."

"What do you mean?" Jenny asked, perplexed.

"Never mind that," Star rushed. "You go talk to the sheriff."

"And take your time, dear," Petunia said. "No need to rush back. I'll handle things here."

Heather stood up, tightening her hold around Tootsie.

"I better go too. I'll walk out with you."

The two girls walked down the steps of the café and paused on the street.

"What are those old biddies sniggering about?" Jenny asked.

"Matchmaking. They think Adam has a thing for you."

Jenny's face blanched.

"Seriously? Adam Hopkins hasn't spared a kind word for me since I got here."

"But you like him, don't you?"

81

Heather asked cagily. "I've seen how you look at him. Your eyes follow him around the room."

"You need to get your eyes checked," Jenny snorted. "I thought Molly was the one with the glasses."

Heather shrugged and waved goodbye but she had a faint smile on her lips. Jenny walked down the street to the police station. The clerk at the front desk called out a greeting.

"Hey Jenny! When are you bringing some of your cheesecake for us? The whole town's raving about it."

"I'll bring some by next time,

Nora," Jenny promised. "Is the sheriff around?"

"He's in his office," the clerk said. "Let me check if he's free."

"I think he's expecting me," Jenny said, heading toward the door.

She knocked once and pushed the door open. Adam Hopkins sat with one foot on a chair. The top button of his uniform was undone and he was in the process of pulling up a pant leg. Jenny's arrival startled him.

"What's this? Nora!" he roared. "Get this woman out of here."

"We need to talk!" Jenny exclaimed, her hands on her hips.

"Get the hell outta here. I'm busy."

"Busy slacking off?" Jenny rolled her eyes. "Must be nice...putting your feet up in the middle of the day. Now that you've done your job and arrested an innocent."

Nora from the front desk rushed in and looked at Adam with concern.

"Can I get you something, Sheriff?"

"Get this woman out of here."

"I'm not moving until you talk to me. I demand an explanation."

"I don't have to tell you anything," Adam spit out.

"Aren't you supposed to serve the people of this town?"

"You are not one of them," Adam pounced. "You are just a visitor."

"That's what you think! I'm here to stay."

"Stay. Leave. Do what you want. Just get out of here now. I'm on my lunch hour."

Jenny scanned Adam's desk. It was Spartan and devoid any evidence of food.

"Where is your lunch?"

"I've sent someone out to get me a sandwich," Adam said wearily.

"One of your minions?" Jenny

asked.

"You won't let up, will you?" Adam sighed.

"Not unless you talk to me and tell me what's going on."

Adam muttered under his breath and unscrewed a bottle of pills. Jenny narrowed her eyes and tried to read the label but she was too far away. Adam popped two pills in his mouth and chased them down with a sip of water.

"How can I help you, Miss King?"

"You can start by telling me why you arrested my aunt."

"She wasn't arrested," Adam sighed. "We just brought her in

for questioning."

"But why? You could have talked to her at her home, or at her gallery. Why did you have to bring her in like a common criminal?"

A muscle worked in Adam's jaw.

"I don't have to explain myself to you, but I'll answer this one time. We needed to show her some stuff. She needed to be here for that."

"You mean you wanted to show her the man's photo?"

Adam stared in the distance but didn't say a word.

"Who is the dead man?"

"This is an ongoing investigation. Any information we find out is strictly off limits."

"So you don't know who he is."

"I can neither confirm nor deny that."

"What's with the mumbo jumbo?" Jenny demanded. "You have no idea who that dead man is or how he got here. Why not admit it?"

"Why don't you go back to your café and bake a cake or something?" Adam asked.

"You think that's all I'm good for?"

"Just get off my back, Jenny!" Adam boomed.

"Do I need to hire a lawyer for Star?"

"Does she need one?" he raised an eyebrow.

"I think she does, especially if you are going to drag her out here for the silliest reasons."

"Your aunt came willingly."

"Did she have a choice?" Jenny cried.

"Yes, she did," Adam nodded. "We asked for her assistance with an ongoing case and she agreed to come here and help us."

"So she's not a suspect in your case, then?"

"I can't answer that."

"I suppose that's a yes," Jenny mumbled to herself.

She looked up at Adam and considered her next question. Adam beat her to it.

"Why don't you let us do our job? Stop meddling in police work."

"I'm just looking out for my aunt," Jenny bristled. "Or trying to."

"Your aunt has nothing to worry about if she is innocent."

"Star said you found one of her brushes."

Adam shrugged and stayed quiet.

"How do you know it's hers? She's not the only one in Pelican Cove who likes to paint, you know. I've seen plenty of people around with sketchbooks, trying to paint the ocean or the marshes."

"This one belonged to her," Adam stressed. "She confirmed it."

"She could have been mistaken," Jenny argued.

"You should talk to your aunt about it," Adam sighed.

Nora knocked on the door and handed over a paper bag.

"Your lunch, Sheriff!"

"You ordered lunch from the café?" Jenny asked. "What did

you get?"

"I've had lunch at the Boardwalk Café every day for years," Adam grunted. "Long before you got here."

He unwrapped his sandwich and bit into it. Something juicy burst into his mouth and he looked up in surprise.

"This is not Petunia's chicken salad!"

"I tweaked the recipe," Jenny said shyly. "Do you like it?"

"It's tart and sweet at the same time. What is it?"

"Strawberries," Jenny supplied. "Fresh from the local farms."

"You have a gift," Adam conceded as he chewed on his chicken salad sandwich. "Folks at the party were raving over your cake."

"I hope the Newburys were happy with our catering," Jenny mused. "We haven't had a chance to ask them yet."

"Ada Newbury is almost impossible to please," Adam snorted. "I wouldn't hold my breath if I were you."

"Petunia said as much," Jenny nodded. "We are hoping other people in town will notice."

Adam held up the sandwich he was eating.

"You have my vote, Jenny King."

Jenny's smile transformed her face.

"So can I tell Star she has nothing to worry about?"

"As long as she's innocent…" Adam popped the last piece of his sandwich in his mouth and wiped his face with a paper napkin. He wadded it up and threw it at a trash can in the corner.

"How long have you known Star?" Jenny asked. "You believe she could do something like this?"

"Star's a bit whimsical," Adam mused, "but I doubt she's the criminal type."

He held up a hand as Jenny relaxed in her chair.

"My personal opinion doesn't count. I have a job to do, and I have to follow procedure."

Jenny stood up, tired of going back and forth with the sheriff. She had learnt nothing new about the dead man. It seemed like Adam Hopkins wasn't going to be forthcoming.

"I have to go."

Adam didn't make any effort to get up.

"Remember what I said. Don't interfere in police business. Let us do our jobs. You concentrate on rustling up some new sandwiches for the café."

Jenny's face began to turn red.

Adam picked up a file and began rifling through the pages. Jenny stomped her foot and turned around. She sailed out of the police station without saying goodbye to Nora.

"What did he say?" Petunia asked as soon as she entered the café.

"Adam Hopkins is the most odious man I have ever met!" Jenny fumed.

"Worse than William?" Star asked, referring to Jenny's estranged husband.

"They are all alike. Men!"

"Why don't you set yourself down?" Petunia wheedled, pulling up a chair.

She stole a glance at Star and the two old ladies held back a giggle.

"He says I should stay in the kitchen and work on my recipes."

"That rascal!" Star exclaimed. "How dare he criticize your cooking."

"Actually, he liked my new chicken salad sandwich..."

"Maybe you should take one for him next time," Star said. "Or how about a nice warm muffin?"

"I'm going to get to the bottom of this," Jenny said in a huff.

She pulled on her apron and began whipping butter for frosting.

Chapter 5

Jenny walked on the beach the next morning, mulling over the last few days. She reverted to brooding whenever she was alone nowadays. She raised the volume on her phone, hoping the music would drown out her thoughts.

A salty breeze blew around her, bringing some spray along with it. The waves crashed on the shore, and the golden rays of the rising sun blended with the aquamarine of the water. Jenny told herself she was blessed to be living in this paradise.

Jenny paused to catch her breath and stared out at the ocean. She planted her feet firmly in the sand

and started doing stretches. They were supposed to calm her. Jenny found her feet slipping in the sand and snorted with sarcasm. Life was a slippery slope, just like the wet sand.

Jenny had spent the last two decades taking care of the two men in her life. She had been the perfect Mom, chairing PTA groups and baking cupcakes. She had been the chic wife for William, entertaining his colleagues and clients, keeping everyone happy. She had sent Nick off to college with a smile and sighed with relief, dreaming of the Caribbean vacation William had promised her.

William had come through alright.

He had promised she wouldn't get a penny if she made a fuss. Jenny knew a lot of lawyers but they were all William's friends. One of the wives had reached out to her and given her a contact number. Jenny's loving home had suddenly started closing in around her. She had packed a bag and moved to a hotel. Star's offer had been a godsend.

Jenny realized she owed a lot to her aunt. She would do anything to protect her from this latest crisis.

Jenny picked up a stick embedded in the sand and flung it wide. She was acting out of habit. It was a moment before she realized her beloved Cookie wasn't with her.

That had been the last straw. Fortunately for Jenny, Nick had already turned eighteen so William couldn't control whether he met his mother. But he had retained custody of their dog, an aging terrier who was blind in one eye. William considered him part of the estate. Jenny crossed her fingers and hoped her lawyer would have some good news for her.

Star was sitting at the kitchen table sipping coffee.

"You seem cool," Jenny commented as she pulled up a chair and poured herself a cup.

"It's a beautiful morning," Star said gaily. "I'm going to paint the marshes today."

Star painted the ocean, the bay and the salt marshes around her in every season and at every hour of the day. These seascapes were quite popular with the tourists that thronged the area in the summer. Star had a small art gallery where she sold these pictures. Spring was a busy season for her. It was the time when she built a steady catalog for the summer rush.

"Are you setting up your easel somewhere?" Jenny asked curiously.

Star was a versatile artist. When the weather permitted, she set up her easel outdoors. Otherwise, she painted from photos she took with her cell phone. She was always clicking pictures of the things around her.

"High of 60s today," Star nodded. "What are you up to, Jenny?"

"Just the usual day at the café," Jenny shrugged. "I might try out a new frosting."

"The Boardwalk Café is a landmark," Star commented. "But your efforts are also being noticed. Keep at it, girl."

The Boardwalk Café had become Jenny's lifeline. She couldn't imagine what she would do without it.

Star stood up and began stuffing

things in her satchel. Jenny watched her aunt stuff a palette and some brushes into the bag and something clicked.

"Tell me something," she said urgently. "Why did the cops think the paintbrush belonged to you?"

"It's got my initials on it," Star said. "See?"

She pulled a brush out of the bag and showed it to Jenny. The letters R and K were etched into the brush.

"Do you always do that?" Jenny asked.

"I keep losing my brushes. This helps me get some of them back. They cost a pretty penny."

"How many people know you mark your brushes this way?"

Star shrugged.

"Everyone knows, I guess. Why? Is it important?"

"I don't know," Jenny admitted.

Jenny grabbed a quick shower and dressed for the work day. Her wardrobe had undergone a drastic change since she came to Pelican Cove. She had put away all her suits and sweater sets after a month in town. Now she went for a more casual look. Denim had become her new friend.

Petunia was flipping pancakes when Jenny entered the café kitchen. She greeted the pleasant

older woman and picked up a
fresh pot of coffee.

"How are you, Captain Charlie?"
she smiled at a crusty old sailor
who was one of their regulars.

He ran a boat charter business,
renting out kayaks and canoes
and offering guided bird watching
and fishing tours.

Captain Charlie forked some
pancakes drenched in syrup and
held them up.

"Taking care of my sweet tooth,"
he grinned. "Petunia says this is
your recipe."

Jenny had added in a healthy
dose of cinnamon to the pancake
batter. She believed in spicing

things up.

"Come back for lunch," she urged. "I'm making crab salad today."

Captain Charlie patted his stomach and licked his lips. His smile turned into a frown.

"What's this I hear about your aunt getting arrested?"

Jenny's good mood evaporated in an instant.

"They wanted to ask her some questions."

"I've known your aunt forty some years, missy," Captain Charlie said. "Whatever it is they are trying to pin on her, she didn't do it."

"Thanks," Jenny said simply.

She was still amazed by how the people in the town looked out for each other.

"Maybe I should talk to that Hopkins boy," Captain Charlie said, scratching his head. "He's getting a bit too big for his britches."

"He's just doing his job, I guess," Jenny shrugged.

Heather walked in, followed by her grandmother. Betty Sue was craning her neck, looking for someone, while her knitting needles clacked in rhythm.

"Is your aunt here?" she asked Jenny.

Jenny shook her head.

"She's out painting by the marshes today."

"Good," Betty Sue expelled.

She strode into the kitchen and Heather followed her like a puppy. Tootsie was nowhere in sight.

Jenny went around the deck, refilling coffee and chatting to the few guests. She walked in on Betty Sue and Petunia with their heads together.

"What's the buzz?" she whispered to Heather.

"They are talking about your aunt," she said.

Petunia looked up and patted the chair next to her.

"Sit down," she ordered Jenny. "Now listen up. You know your aunt's a bit different. She can't be bothered about stuff. I don't think she's taking this police business seriously."

Jenny thought for a minute and nodded. Star seemed a bit too composed.

"You need to get cracking," Betty Sue declared, pointing a finger at Jenny.

"I talked to the sheriff yesterday," Jenny protested. "He knows I'm looking out for my aunt."

"That's fine," Petunia said.

"What's next on your list? Have you drawn up a plan yet?"

"I thought you were talking about the Spring Fest," Jenny burst out. "Don't we have to come up with a new recipe for it?"

"That too," Petunia said. "I'm sure you'll come up with something, Jenny."

"Should it be a savory or a dessert?" Jenny asked.

She was trying to distract the old ladies. Petunia took the bait.

"One of each, I think. Something simple though. Like that strawberry chicken salad you made yesterday."

"Won't that go bad in the sun?"
Betty Sue asked.

Petunia's chins wobbled as she
shook her head.

"Jenny doesn't use mayo. She
uses Greek yogurt. That's her
secret ingredient."

"Why haven't I tried this salad of
yours?" Betty Sue demanded.

"Check in the refrigerator, Jenny,"
Petunia said. "We might have
some left over from yesterday."

"It's time for my morning snack,"
Betty Sue nodded. "I've been up
since five."

Jenny poked her head into the
refrigerator and pulled out a bowl

of chicken salad. She toasted some bread lightly and started assembling a sandwich for Betty Sue.

"Do you want one too?" she asked Heather.

Heather leaned against the door, staring out on the street.

"Chris is taking me to the Steakhouse tonight."

"Wow. Isn't that fancy?" Jenny asked.

There were a limited number of establishments in Pelican Cove. People had set ideas about where to go for what occasion. The Boardwalk Café was the place to go for breakfast or lunch. You went to the Rusty Anchor for a pint at the end of the day. Ethan's Crab Shack offered the catch of the day, fried perfectly. But there was only one place you went to for a special date and that was the Steakhouse.

Heather was looking troubled.

"Why do you think he's taking me there? The Rusty Anchor's good enough."

"Are you actually complaining?" Jenny asked Heather. "Just put on a pretty dress and enjoy your evening."

"Chris and I...we are just hanging out."

"You mean you're not dating?"

Jenny asked.

Heather and Chris were joined at the hip. They got along like a house on fire. Jenny could tell they cared for each other.

"It's all been casual so far," Heather said. "Why is he taking me to a fancy place all of a sudden?"

"Maybe he has something to celebrate?" Jenny speculated. "Do you have an anniversary or birthday coming up?"

Heather shook her head.

"He was working on closing a deal."

Chris worked part time as a

realtor in addition to putting in some hours at his family's seafood market.

"Well then," Jenny soothed, tucking her hair behind her ear. "Maybe he earned a fat commission and wants to splurge."

Heather seemed mollified.

"You're right. What else could it be?"

Chapter 6

The buzz about the murder died down after a while. People stopped speculating about it. It was no longer the topic of the hour at the Boardwalk Café. Jenny mentally heaved a sigh of relief. She was tired of being consoled by strangers. People she didn't know came up to her and told her they believed in her aunt. It gave her an idea of how the community could come together in a period of crisis.

"You never told me about your special date," Jenny said to Heather one morning.

Petunia and Betty Sue were sipping coffee on the deck,

enjoying the warmth of the mid-morning sun. People strolling on the boardwalk waved at the two old ladies as they walked past. Heather was munching on a muffin as Jenny frosted a cake.

"It's what I was afraid of," Heather said sadly. "He wants to speed things up."

"Are you moving in together?" Jenny asked with excitement.

Heather sucked in a breath. She looked right and left before she hissed in Jenny's ear.

"Are you mad?"

"Isn't that the next step in your relationship?" Jenny asked, bewildered.

"People don't 'move in' in Pelican Cove. My grandma will have a fit if she hears you."

"It's 2018, you know," Jenny said lightly. "The world has changed in the last 100 years or so."

"How long have you been here, Jenny?" Heather asked, rolling her eyes. "Time may have passed, but we still follow the principles laid down by my great great great great grandpa Morse."

"When was that again?"

"1837. For all intents and purposes, we still live in Victorian times."

"So you want a ring on your finger first," Jenny nodded.

"That's always a smart move."

"Chris hinted at it," Heather said, making a face. "I don't get what the rush is."

"You're in your 30s, right?" Jenny asked delicately. "Don't you want to settle down?"

The café door opened and a short, squat man came in. His copper hair was the same color as his mustache and sideburns. They matched the pockmarks and red welts on his face courtesy of years of acne. He smiled when he saw Jenny and gave her a salute.

"Hey Jenny," he called out, handing over a bundle. "Got lots of goodies for you today. Looks important."

Jenny took the bundle of papers from the man and blushed as she saw her lawyer's letterhead. Did everyone in town know her business?

Kevin Brown, Pelican Cove's one and only mailman, gave her a sympathetic look.

"I don't show them around to everyone, Jenny."

"Thanks," Jenny mumbled. "Would you like a cupcake?"

"Best offer I got all day," Kevin smiled. "Is it a new recipe?"

"Orange and strawberry," Jenny nodded. "I am trying it out for the

Spring Fest."

"How's it going, Kevin?" Heather asked. "Haven't seen you at the Rusty Anchor in a while."

The mailman chatted with Heather and Jenny. He wanted to know how Star was dealing with the police threat.

"That Hopkins boy has finally come to his senses," Betty Sue Morse called out, knitting furiously.

She was juggling green and orange balls of wool, alternating between the two colors. Jenny wondered if she should take up knitting as a hobby. Betty Sue could get her started, teach her the basics.

Jenny lounged in a chair on her aunt's front porch later that evening, staring at the ocean. She rubbed the small charm that reminded her of her son. It was a tiny heart engraved with her name. Nick had given it to her on his 10th birthday. Nick was enjoying freshman year in college and was too busy to come visit.

"How are you really doing, Mom?" he had asked her on the phone.

Jenny had been touched at his concern. She had a sudden urge to take Cookie for a walk. Her eyes filled up as she thought of everything she had left behind. She was dealing with much more than an empty nest.

A yellow Labrador came bounding down the beach, snapping her out of her thoughts.

"Tank! Tank! Stop right there."

A tall man came into her line of vision, leaning on a cane and trying to hurry behind the dog. He grabbed the dog's leash and brought him up short.

Jenny felt a familiar pair of blue eyes trained on her. Even in the fading twilight, she recognized the man easily.

"Sheriff," she said stiffly.

"Jenny!" he exclaimed. "What are you doing here?"

"I live here," Jenny replied sullenly.

"Of course," Adam Hopkins muttered, dragging the dog behind him. "This is Tank."

He turned to the dog and said softly, "Say Hi to the lady, Tank."

The dog cowered behind Adam and began whining.

"He's a big boy," Jenny said, walking toward the dog. "How old is he?"

"We are both getting on in years," Adam sniffed. "Not as young as we used to be."

Jenny patted the dog and stroked him behind his ears. He stopped whining and sat down in the sand, offering up a paw.

"He hasn't done that in months," Adam said, surprised. "You must have a calming effect on him."

"I miss my dog," Jenny admitted. "Maybe I can take Tank for a walk sometime?"

Adam noticed how wistful she sounded.

"As long as he lets you do that," he said. "Tank's having some behavioral issues. He doesn't let anyone get close."

"What's wrong with him?" Jenny asked. "He looks quite healthy."

"We were both scarred by the

war," Adam said, nodding toward his leg. "Some wounds are not visible."

"Are you saying he has PTSD or something?" Jenny laughed nervously.

"That's exactly what he has," Adam admitted. "He's been through a rough time. Now it's my turn to take care of him."

"I didn't know you were a soldier," Jenny said with wonder. "Were you deployed?"

"I was in the Middle East," Adam told her. "They finally put me out to pasture. And here I am, back home in Pelican Cove."

"You sound like you had an

127

interesting life," Jenny said.

She was envious. Apparently, Adam Hopkins was not the country bumpkin she had thought he was.

"Do you bring him for a walk here every day?" Jenny asked.

"Not really," Adam laughed. "He decides where he wants to go."

Adam said goodbye after that. Jenny wondered if she had misjudged him.

Jenny hummed a tune as she poured coffee for her customers the next day. Cherry trees were blooming around town and the sun was shining. Business was ramping up at the café and

Petunia told her to put up a 'Now Hiring' sign on the bulletin board.

"Why don't we post it online?" she asked.

"We don't need those fancy computers to get some help," Petunia dismissed. "One of the kids will read the board and come in to work."

The phone in the kitchen rang just then and Petunia asked her to go get it. Betty Sue Morse had arrived and the two old ladies were sipping their mid-morning cuppa out on the deck.

"Where is your aunt?" Betty Sue called out. "She was supposed to meet us here today."

Jenny stepped out of the kitchen in a daze. Her face was white with shock.

"What's wrong?" Petunia's two chins wobbled as she clutched her bosom.

Betty Sue stopped knitting and leaned forward.

"Speak up, girl."

Jenny pointed a finger toward the kitchen. "Star!" she burst out. "That was Star. They just arrested her."

The two old women stared at each other and turned toward Jenny.

"Go find Jason Stone," Betty Sue snapped. "Tell him I sent you."

"Who's that?" Jenny asked. "I need to go bail out Star."

"Jason's a lawyer," Petunia explained. "He's done some work for your aunt before."

"He's the only lawyer in town," Betty Sue went on.

She had started knitting again. Her needles clacked in their usual rhythm as she peered at Jenny.

"I'm on my way," Jenny said grimly, pulling off her apron and throwing it on a chair.

"He's on Main Street right opposite the police station," Betty Sue called out.

Jenny waved a hand in the air,

letting them know she had heard. She noticed the 'Stone & Stone' sign as soon as she walked past the library.

She pushed open the heavy glass door and looked around for a secretary. A tall man with a head full of coal black hair lounged in a leather chair inside a room. He beckoned her to come in.

"What can I do for you, Jenny?"

"You know my name?" Jenny asked, astonished.

Jason Stone managed to look hurt.

"Have you forgotten me already?"

Jenny didn't have time for this

nonsense.

"Please. This is urgent. I am looking for Jason Stone. I am in need of his services."

"You really don't remember, do you?" he chuckled. "We went out on a couple of dates, back in the day."

Jenny had spent a few summers in Pelican Cove as a teenager. She vaguely remembered a melting ice cream cone and an attractive black haired, pimple faced teen in leather pants. Was that the guy sitting before her now?

"Now I do..." she smiled. "Vaguely."

Jason pointed to a chair and urged her to sit.

"I can see you're all riled up so let's get down to business first."

"They got her. They arrested my aunt. We need to go bail her out."

"What did Star do now?" Jason joked. "I didn't see any water cannons in town."

Jenny decided she didn't care for his sense of humor. It was misplaced at best.

"I don't know why they arrested her. That's what we have to find out."

Jason Stone finally sensed Jenny's mood and stood up. They walked briskly to the police station.

"They brought your aunt in," Nora, the front desk clerk, confirmed as soon as they went in. "They are booking her now."

"Let me handle this," Jason said grimly.

Jenny paced the lobby, waiting for some news. She spied Adam coming out of the small corner room. He went into his office. She rushed in without paying any heed to Nora's warning.

"How dare you!" she screamed at the sheriff. "Why have you arrested my aunt? What are the charges?"

"She's being charged with

murder," Adam said grimly. "She's the sole suspect in the case, Jenny. She still can't explain why the victim had her paintbrush."

"She doesn't even know the guy!" Jenny exclaimed.

"That's what she says," Adam agreed. "But criminals often lie, in my experience."

"You take that back!" Jenny roared. "Star's not a criminal. She has been a model citizen of this town for the last forty something years."

"She has a record, you know."

Jenny was speechless. She hadn't known that.

"You can't hold that against her. Whatever she did before this is immaterial. She did not commit this crime. You have no proof."

"The court will decide that."

"All you have is some flimsy evidence. It's not going to be enough."

Adam closed his eyes and massaged his temples.

"I know you're worried about her, Jenny. Why don't you go get a good lawyer?"

"She has a lawyer," Jenny said.

She stormed out as she remembered Jason Stone. It took three hours for Jason to work his magic. Jenny finally walked out of the police station with Star. Her aunt looked haggard as she leaned against her.

"We're going home now," Jenny promised.

"Let's go to the Boardwalk Café first," Star said weakly. "The girls must be worried."

Petunia and Betty Sue Morse were sitting at the same table where Jenny had left them. An empty coffee pot sat next to a pile of dirty cups. They had been joined by Heather and Molly from the library.

"Star!" they exclaimed as soon as they spied Jenny walking up the steps with her aunt.

"I'll get you a sandwich," Petunia said, getting up.

She was back with two plates. The group refused to talk until Jenny and Star had eaten something.

Betty Sue Morse rapped the table as Star wolfed down her last bite.

"Are you going to get to the bottom of this, Jenny?"

Chapter 7

Petunia closed the café a few
hours early that day. She handed
over a brown paper bag to
Captain Charlie as she turned him
away.

"We got to hunker down and take
some serious action," she told
him.

"Did that Hopkins boy really
arrest Star?"

"So you heard already," Petunia
sighed. "He did, Captain Charlie.
Jenny went and got Jason Stone
to bail her out."

"Tell her to hang in there,"
Captain Charlie said as he peeked
into the brown paper bag.

"There's plenty for me here. You gals take care of Star now."

He walked down the steps of the café and crossed the boardwalk. Petunia saw him heading to the beach and went inside with determination.

"Start talking, Jenny," she commanded as she sat down next to Betty Sue. "What's the plan?"

Jenny was feeling flustered. Star came to her rescue.

"Relax! Adam's just doing his job. I guess he had to bring someone in to show them he's doing something."

"He said you had a record," Jenny said meekly.

141

Star didn't bat an eyelid.

"Of course I have a record. I was an activist back in the day."

"What for?" Molly asked curiously.

"It was the 60s," Star shrugged. "We protested about pretty much everything."

"Were you in an anti-war protest?" Jenny asked.

"Anti-war, civil rights, women's lib, you name it…"

"Your aunt's supported the pelicans and the whales too," Betty Sue said proudly. "She's one of a kind."

"That was several years ago. It

doesn't have any bearing on the crime today."

"They always bring the ex-cons in first," Star said in a matter of fact way.

"How can you be so cool about this?" Jenny quizzed. "Bail is just a reprieve. We need to prove you didn't do this."

"Isn't that the job of the police?" Heather asked.

She was clutching Tootsie in her arms again. She had run back to the inn in Jenny's absence and found Tootsie whining in a corner. Tootsie refused to eat her lunch so Heather brought the poodle back with her and fed her at the cafe. Between Heather and Betty Sue, Tootsie was used to being pampered. She always got her way. Petunia warned Heather to keep the poodle away from the kitchen.

"If the police were doing their job, they would never have taken Star in."

Petunia seconded Betty Sue's statement.

"You're the smart one here, Jenny. What's our next step?"

"I'm as clueless as you are," Jenny protested. "I'm not an investigator."

"Maybe not," Betty Sue reasoned. "But you have city smarts. And you went to college."

Jenny wiped off the specials board and picked up a piece of chalk. She needed to write things down. She always worked better with lists.

"Let's write down what we know," she said.

"We don't know the name of the victim," Molly Henderson said primly. "He's a John Doe as they say in the movies."

Jenny wrote 'Name' on the board and added 'Unknown' in front of it.

"Address is also unknown," Heather spoke up.

"Purpose of Visit," Betty Sue supplied.

"Person Visiting," Petunia said, getting into the rhythm.

"All of these are Unknown," Jenny said as she updated the board. "So we essentially know nothing about this person."

"We know how he looks," Star said casually.

"What?" Jenny burst out. "How do we know that?"

"Adam showed me a photo, remember?" Star asked them. "I can draw a sketch based on that."

"You remember his face?" Jenny asked.

Star shrugged.

"All I need is a pencil and some paper, or a crayon. Anything, really."

"I'll go get some," Heather offered.

She set Tootsie down and pulled at her leash.

"Come on Toots."

Jenny made some fresh coffee while Heather was gone, although she wasn't sure if she could handle more caffeine. Her brain was already buzzing with a thousand questions.

Heather was back, clutching paper and pencils, tugging Tootsie behind her.

Star got to work. The girls watched silently as Star's fingers flew across the paper. She had drawn a rough outline within seconds. She finally looked up five minutes later and handed them the paper.

Betty Sue, Petunia, Heather and Jenny stared at the picture that emerged. None of them noticed Molly's face turn white.

The face that stared back at them was ordinary. They were sure of one thing. They had never set eyes on him before.

"He's not from Pelican Cove," Betty Sue declared. "I should

know."

Betty Sue prided herself on knowing everyone in town. She had lived there for 75 years and she hailed from the first family of the island.

"He hasn't come to the cafe," Petunia said strongly. "I would remember a stranger."

"What about you, Star?" Jenny asked. "Have you seen him before?"

Star shook her head.

"Doesn't look familiar to me. I know most people in town. I even remember some of the regular tourists."

Jenny looked around at them.

"What do we do now?"

Molly cleared her throat and stood up.

"I'm sorry, but I have to get back to work."

"Thanks for coming here," Jenny said, giving Molly a hug. "It means a lot to me."

"What's eating her?" Betty Sue whispered as soon as Molly left. "Did you see the sweat beading her brow?"

"Hush, Betty Sue," Petunia said, tapping her friend on the hand. "Pay attention to Jenny."

"Does anyone have any ideas?" Jenny asked.

"Why don't we make copies and show this picture around?" Heather asked.

"That's brilliant, Heather," Jenny said with a smile. "We can post a picture up here on the bulletin board. Maybe you can put one up at the inn."

"Why stop there?" Betty Sue asked. "Take a picture around to all the local shops. Go to Williams' Seafood Market and the Rusty Anchor. Add your phone number at the bottom and ask people to contact you if they know something."

"What about the sheriff?" Jenny mused. "Will he have a problem with this?"

"You'll find out soon enough," Betty Sue snorted. "You're doing nothing wrong."

Star wanted to fill in some color in the picture to make it look more lifelike. She finally handed it over to Jenny.

"Do you have a scanner?" she asked her aunt. "I can scan this and print out copies."

"It's broken," Star told her.

Jenny looked at Heather.

"Don't look at me. We don't even have a computer at the inn.

Grandma won't let me buy one."

"You don't need that machine to keep track of a few guests," Betty Sue began, ready to embark on her hobby horse.

"I'll go to the nearest copy place," Jenny said hastily.

"You'll have to drive over to the next town," Petunia told her. "They have one of those business centers in the mall where that big grocery store is."

"Doesn't the library have a copier?" Star asked.

"Duh!" Jenny said with a laugh. "That should work just fine. How many copies shall I get?"

153

Betty Sue and Heather left with Jenny.

"I haven't done any of my chores today," Heather said.

She was in charge of cleaning the rooms. Their new guests would be checking in later that evening.

"Go with Jenny and bring back a few copies for us," Betty Sue told Heather as she took Tootsie's leash. "I'll give this sweetie her walk and then head home."

"Okay Grandma!" Heather agreed.

Molly was nowhere in sight when they reached the library.

"She went home early," one of the girls who worked at the library told them. "Had a migraine."

"Ohhh..." Jenny sympathized. "Sounds painful."

Jenny got fifty copies of the picture and handed a few over to Heather.

"I wish I could go with you," Heather said wistfully. "But duty calls."

"Don't worry," Jenny patted her on the shoulder. "You've been a big help. I am so glad I have your support."

"You can count on me, Jenny," Heather said, pulling her in for a quick hug.

Jenny went back to the Boardwalk

Café and pinned the picture up on their bulletin board. The notice seeking help was already gone. Jenny wondered if someone had removed it to get rid of the competition. She would put a new one up later.

Petunia was cleaning up in the kitchen. Star was sitting at the table, looking exhausted. Her tie dyed tee shirt looked cheap in the afternoon light. Her face was devoid of any makeup. Her earlobes, one longer than the other, looked odd without their dangling earrings. It looked like the police hadn't waited long enough for her aunt to dress properly.

"Can we go home now, Jenny?"

Star asked.

"I was thinking of handing these out at a couple of places," Jenny said. "Why don't we grab a pint at the Rusty Anchor while we're at it?"

"You go ahead," Star said. "I'm going home."

Jenny felt torn.

"I'll be home soon," she promised. "I think we should show these pictures around as soon as possible."

"You're right, dear," Star conceded. "But I need to lie down."

"Will you promise to take it easy?"

Jenny asked. "I'll make dinner once I get home. I have some chicken breasts marinating in the fridge. Maybe I'll get some fresh shrimp at the market."

As expected, the thought of her favorite shrimp for dinner drew a tired smile out of Star. She urged Jenny to get going.

A gentle breeze was blowing over the ocean. Jenny looked longingly at the boardwalk and promised herself a walk on the beach after dinner. She went out of the front entrance of the café and walked down the street. Her first stop was the seafood market. She ran into Chris as soon as she went in.

"Hey Jenny, how are you holding

up?" he asked when he saw her.

His eyes were laced with concern. Jenny realized the town grapevine had spread the news of Star's arrest far and wide. Everyone in town must know about it, she realized.

"Have you seen this man before?" she asked, showing Chris the victim's picture.

Chris looked at it closely and shook his head. His eyes narrowed as he realized the significance.

"Is this that guy who died?"

Jenny nodded.

"Do you have a board or

159

something where I can pin this up?"

Chris stepped out from behind the counter and took her to a big cork board hanging on the wall. He pulled off some old flyers and put the picture up in a prominent position.

"Can you ask people to give it a glance?" she asked.

"I won't have to," Chris assured her. "Almost every person coming in checks out the board."

"How was your dinner date at the Steakhouse?" Jenny asked, genuinely interested.

"Did Heather tell you anything?" Chris asked.

His ears had turned red when Jenny asked him about their date. Jenny thought it was cute.

"Don't forget the Boardwalk Café when you're looking for a caterer," she winked.

"Huh?" Chris asked, looking bewildered.

"Never mind," Jenny said, taking pity on him.

Guys could be so clueless.

"Got any of your famous shrimp?"

"Of course," Chris said. "The catch just came in. I've got some already peeled and deveined."

"I'll take a pound of that please,"

Jenny said.

She would use the same marinade she had used for the chicken, tequila and lime. It was her aunt's favorite. A nice chicken and shrimp dinner with some herbed rice and veggies would cheer Star up. They could have the orange strawberry cupcakes later for dessert.

"Why don't you leave some more here?" Chris said, pointing to the stack of pictures in Jenny's hand. "I'll ask some of the watermen to pin them up near the dock. Who knows, maybe the guy came here by boat?"

"Good idea!" Jenny said brightly.

She handed over a few pictures to Chris and set off for the Rusty Anchor.

Eddie Cotton greeted her as soon as she entered the pub.

"Why aren't you home taking care of your aunt?" he asked.

"This is my last stop before heading home," Jenny promised.

She handed over some pictures and asked Eddie to show them around.

"Haven't set eyes on this one," Eddie said before she could ask him a question. "I never forget a face."

Jenny pulled up a stool and

leaned against the bar. She talked to a few people as they entered the pub. She called it a day after some time and trudged home.

Chapter 8

Star rallied around a bit after dinner. Jenny made sure she was settled in front of the TV with some peppermint tea. She took a wrap and went out for the walk she had promised herself.

Roses bloomed in the garden next door. Seaview was a three storied house with large wraparound porches facing the sea. It had been for sale since Jenny came to Pelican Cove. A gardener came in every few days but the yard was beginning to look run down. The motion sensing lights at Seaview came on as Jenny walked past. She saw a familiar figure in the distance.

Tank trotted up to her but cowered when she tried to pat him.

"Hello," Adam called out.

He was limping a bit more than usual. Jenny wondered if his condition was permanent.

"Looks like we have a storm coming in," he said. "My leg always lets me know."

"Does it hurt a lot?" Jenny asked.

"Nothing a few pills can't fix."

"I hear they can be habit forming," Jenny said.

She almost bit her lip as the words slipped from her mouth.

She didn't mean to imply Adam was addicted to his medicine.

Surprisingly, Adam didn't seem to take offense.

"It's a line I try hard not to cross," he admitted.

Jenny said goodbye and walked on. She wondered if Adam would come to her beach for a walk every day. There were plenty of beaches in the town of Pelican Cove but many of them were rugged and strewn with rocks. The beach her aunt's house was on was a smooth stretch of two miles facing the ocean.

Jenny had a smile on her face the next day as she whipped the batter for some pancakes.

"Looks like you had a good night," Petunia remarked. "How's your aunt doing?"

"She's okay. I convinced her to stay at home today. She can paint off some of her photos."

"She's got plenty of those," Petunia nodded, her chins jiggling in tandem. "Don't forget to ask people about that picture on the bulletin board."

"I won't," Jenny promised.

Captain Charlie came in for coffee and a muffin. He looked around for Star.

"She's at home today," Jenny told

him.

"That's hard to believe," Captain Charlie snorted. "Probably rushed off somewhere soon as you turned your back."

Jenny shrugged. Her aunt wasn't a captive. She could go out if she wanted to.

"Have you seen this man before, Captain Charlie?"

She gave a quick account of how they got the picture.

"Can't say I have," Captain Charlie shook his head. "Have you got any more of those? I'll put one up in my office."

Jenny asked the same question to

the guests as she poured coffee and filled breakfast orders. She spotted Kevin the mailman walking down the street on his rounds and suddenly remembered her unopened mail. Had she taken it home with her?

Kevin came into the café an hour later.

"How about some of that famous coffee?" he asked Jenny. "And one banana nut muffin, please."

"Is that to go?" Jenny asked.

Kevin thought for a minute and shook his head.

"You know what? I think I'll have it here. I can take a break now."

Jenny took over the coffee and muffin and let Kevin get started. He gave her his usual salute and took a large bite of the muffin.

"Delicious! I don't know how we survived before you came to town."

Jenny let him make some small talk and pointed toward the bulletin board. Kevin took a deep sip of his coffee and gave her a sympathetic look.

"I heard about your aunt. I am so sorry. Star is such a force around town."

"Do you recognize this guy?" Jenny asked. "You must get to every nook and corner of the island on your rounds. Did you come across him anywhere?"

Kevin stood up and walked to the board. He looked at the picture from either side. Jenny felt some hope spring within her. Kevin asked her to pull it off the board so he could have a better look. Jenny went in and brought out a fresh print.

Kevin took it out in the sun and peered at it closely.

"Never set eyes on the guy," he said. "Are you handing these out to people? Why don't I take a few?"

Jenny handed him a few copies when he left.

"Who *is* this guy?" Jenny wailed later as she drank a fresh cup of coffee.

Betty Sue and Heather had come along for their mid-morning break. The group was assembled on the deck out back. Black clouds lined the horizon and the waves seemed a bit stronger.

"Storm coming in," Betty Sue said.

"That's what Adam said."

"When did you meet Adam?" Heather asked with a gleam in her eyes.

"I ran into him on the beach last night."

173

"What were you doing there, Jenny?" Petunia asked. "Didn't you go home to take care of your aunt?"

"I did!" Jenny assured her friends. "I went for a walk after dinner."

"Wonder what Adam was doing there," Betty Sue said cagily. "It's not like he lives in that side of town."

Jenny's thoughts were occupied by the man in the picture.

"He's a ghost," Jenny said.

Molly Henderson joined them.

"I'm taking an early lunch. Can I have one of your famous chicken salad sandwiches, Jenny?"

"Jenny just made a new batch," Petunia said proudly. "People really love them."

Jenny went inside to rustle up Molly's sandwich.

"What's the latest?" Molly asked the others. "Anything new happen in Pelican Cove?"

"We are talking about that guy in the picture," Heather spoke up. "Not a single person in town recognizes him."

"What's the Spring Fest going to be like this year?" Molly asked, changing the subject.

"The Spring Fest will be fine," Betty Sue dismissed. "There are more urgent things underfoot."

175

"Did you put up a picture in the library?" Petunia asked suddenly. "Jenny's been handing these out at local businesses, but we completely forgot the library."

"I don't think it will make any difference," Molly argued. "Hardly anyone goes to the library these days."

"What are you talking about, girl?" Betty Sue demanded. "Other than the Boardwalk Café, the library is the one place in town everyone visits."

"Young or old..." Petunia added.

"Maybe he was a tourist, just driving through town." Heather scratched her head. "He could have been on his way north into Chincoteague, or Delaware."

"Or he could be one of those salesmen," Petunia said, "selling new roofs or something."

"What's going on?" Jenny asked, placing Molly's food in front of her.

Molly picked up a potato chip and bit into it.

"That man," Petunia explained to Jenny. "We are talking about how none of the people in town seem to know him."

"And Molly needs to put up his mug shot at the library," Heather added.

177

The four women trained their eyes on Molly, waiting for her to say yes.

"Alright, alright, I'll take care of it. Now let me eat my lunch."

The group broke up after that. Jenny placed a couple of pictures on the table in front of Molly.

"Thanks, Molls."

Molly stuffed the pictures in her bag.

Hours later, Jenny and Petunia were ready to close the café and go home. There was a tapping sound on the wooden steps and Jenny spied Adam coming up the stairs.

"We are closed but I can rustle up a sandwich if you're hungry," Jenny said with a smile.

"I'm not here to eat," Adam said grimly. "We need to talk."

He looked imposing in his sheriff's uniform. Jenny stared into his glowering blue eyes as all six feet two of him towered over her.

"What's wrong?" she asked, pulling at her necklace and rubbing one of the charms in it.

Adam jabbed a finger at the bulletin board.

"This! You're making a mockery of my investigation."

"How so?" Jenny asked, placing

one hand on her hip. "I'm just trying to gather some information."

"That's my job!" Adam snapped.

"I'm just asking people if they saw this man around town."

"Where did you get this picture anyway?"

"My aunt drew it from the photo you showed her."

"It's almost an exact likeness," Adam admitted grudgingly.

"Have you found out who he is?"

"We are making inquiries," Adam said. "I can't tell you anything more."

"I'm not asking you, am I?" Jenny said pertly. "But I can ask people in town. I don't think I'm breaking any law by doing that."

"You are meddling in something that isn't your business."

"I need to protect my aunt. You arrested her on the most flimsy evidence. I'm just making sure it won't happen again."

"You can't dictate what the police do," Adam warned.

"What if I find someone who had a motive to kill this man? Will you drop the charges against Star?"

Adam pursed his lips.

"Let me answer that," Jenny said

briskly. "You will have to. And that's what I am trying to do."

"You are a civilian. This could be dangerous, Jenny."

"There's no danger here," Jenny dismissed. "I don't see the harm in showing a picture around."

"And how's that working for you?" Adam raised his eyebrows.

"I'm just getting started," Jenny said.

"I think what you're doing is silly."

"Let's not talk about it then," Jenny bristled. "Good night!"

Petunia stood behind the kitchen door, her mouth hanging open.

She had listened to the whole exchange. She didn't know what to make of it. Adam Hopkins had never been so confrontational with anyone before.

Jenny grilled fish for dinner later that evening. She had poured a glass of Chardonnay for herself and Star. The wine came from Pelican Cove's local winery and was perfect with the sea bass Jenny was cooking.

"Crab season's almost here," Star said as she took a sip. "Wait till you taste our local blue crabs. You're going to love them, Jenny."

"I'm working on a crab dip recipe," Jenny said. "Petunia said

we have full access to the
Bayview Inn's garden. They have
a nice patch of herbs."

"The soft shell crabs are the best.
Ethan does them very well. Have
you been to his crab shack yet?"

"Haven't had the time," Jenny
said. "Let's go there for dinner
sometime."

"Ethan's one handsome hunk,"
Star said.

Jenny rolled her eyes.

"But, he's taken. Unlike his
brother."

"And who is his brother?" Jenny
asked, humoring her aunt.

"Adam, of course!"

"Adam Hopkins?" Jenny asked, fanning herself. "Pelican Cove's too small for two Hopkins men."

"Wait till you meet him, sweetie," Star said cryptically.

The two women laughed and joked over dinner. Jenny grew serious as she dished up a sorbet for their dessert.

"How was your day, Auntie? Are you holding up well?"

Star waved off her concern.

"I finished a canvas I was working on and started painting Seaview. I can do that from our yard. I love painting that house."

"Why is it empty?" Jenny asked curiously. "It's such a gorgeous property. Why hasn't someone snapped it up yet?"

"It's a long story," Star said. "Something bad happened there. People around here think that place is jinxed."

"That's just superstition," Jenny said.

"Most people here come from seafaring families. Sailors are a superstitious bunch."

Jenny's mind drifted to the dead stranger.

"Would you say people here are vigilant?"

"You mean they are gossips?" Star smirked. "We don't have much else to keep us busy."

"Then how is it no one recognizes that dead man? Is it possible he came to Pelican Cove and no one ran into him?"

"He ran into one person alright," Star said, making the double quote sign with her fingers. "The person who sent him to the other world."

"I must have talked to dozens of people, Star."

"Don't you see, Jenny?" Star asked as she drained her wine. "At least one of them is lying."

Chapter 9

Jenny was lost in thought as she frosted some cupcakes a few days later. She had shown the dead man's sketch around town several times. She figured almost every person living in Pelican Cove must have visited the Boardwalk Café in the past few days. Every person coming in had been diligently directed to the bulletin board. Chris at the seafood market or Eddie at the pub hadn't had any luck with the photo either. Jenny wondered what else she could do to help things along.

"This won't do," she said resolutely, shaking her head.

"Are you talking to yourself,

dear?" Petunia asked, coming into the kitchen with a stack of empty plates.

Jenny looked up at Petunia.

"We need to do something more."

"Are you talking about the dead guy?" Petunia asked, catching on. "I think you are taking plenty of effort to find out who he is, or was."

"Whatever I'm doing is not enough, since we are not getting any results. Maybe I need to take a step back and look at it from a distance."

"Huh?"

"Never mind," Jenny mumbled,

already lost in thought again.

"What's on your mind today?" Heather asked as they sipped coffee later that morning.

Betty Sue was knitting with emerald green wool.

"This is going to make a wonderful scarf for someone," she hinted.

"Do you know the beach near the Newbury property?" Jenny asked Heather. "Can anyone go there?"

"It's a private beach," Heather replied. "I doubt the hoi polloi are allowed inside the queen's palace."

"Don't be daft, girl," Betty Sue

snapped.

She turned to look at Jenny.

"There's a small stretch of land there that belongs to the town so it has public access. Ada Newbury had marked her property line with a sign board but the kids keep striking it down."

"So if someone started walking on this beach, they could walk onto the private portion without knowing they were trespassing?"

"I guess so," Betty Sue said. "Tourists go up to the lighthouse all the time and they stray over onto Newbury land. It's Ada Newbury's pet peeve."

"Let's go there, Heather," Jenny

191

said, standing up.

"Wait a minute," Molly said.

She had been busy flipping through a magazine all that time.

"I thought you had let this go, Jenny. Are you still hung up on that guy?"

"Star is still implicated. I can't let this go until I prove her innocence."

Jenny turned to Heather.

"Are you coming or not?"

Heather looked at her grandma.

"You don't need my permission," Betty Sue said. "Anyone would think I make you work like a slave."

Jenny and Heather took the road leading to the Newbury house. The road ran parallel to the beach. The girls could see tall sea grasses and sand stretching to meet the water.

"Stop!" Heather cried as she spied a small turnoff. "This goes to the lighthouse. I remember it now."

They parked the car by the side of the road and started walking.

"How far do we have to go to reach the Newbury estate?" Jenny asked.

"I am not sure where their section of the beach begins," Heather

193

said, pausing to think a bit. "It's a 20-30 minute walk."

Jenny nodded.

"Let's pace ourselves, in that case."

"What are we doing here, Jenny?" Heather asked.

"I'm not sure," she admitted. "I guess I want to see the place where they found the guy. Maybe I'll think of something when we get there."

"But how will we know where they found him?" Heather asked.

"The police use tape to cordon off crime scenes to keep people out."

"You think it's still there?"
Heather frowned. "On the beach?"

Jenny shrugged.

"We won't know until we go look."

"Okay. I don't mind."

It was a warm Spring day and the sun was high over their heads. Jenny felt herself beginning to sweat. She had never focused on fitness in her previous life. Her walks on the beach had improved her stamina a bit but walking in the sun was still tedious. She paused to catch her breath.

An old lighthouse loomed in the distance. The faded red and white bands managed to look striking against the blue backdrop of the ocean and the sky. Jenny could see a couple of figures near the base of the lighthouse. One of the figures had a shock of red hair which tugged at her memory.

"Is that Kevin?" she asked Heather, pointing in the distance.

"Sure looks like him," Heather agreed. "No one else has that shock of red hair in Pelican Cove."

"What's he doing here on this deserted beach?" Jenny panted.

"Delivering mail?" Heather quirked her eyebrow.

"To whom?"

"Jimmy Parsons, I guess. He lives in the lighthouse."

"Someone lives in the lighthouse?" Jenny asked. "Isn't it abandoned?"

"I suppose he doesn't exactly live inside the lighthouse," Heather reasoned. "There's a small cottage next to it. He lives there."

"But why?" Jenny asked.

"The Parsons family owns the lighthouse. They have always taken care of it."

"Does the lighthouse still work?"

"Oh no," Heather said. "It was decommissioned long ago. There's a new light up north."

"Why does he live here then?"

"I don't know. He's a recluse, and a drunk."

Jenny processed this information as the girls walked on. The red headed figure started walking toward them. Kevin gave them his usual salute as he came closer.

"Hello ladies! What are you doing here?"

Heather opened her mouth but paused as Jenny put an arm on her shoulder.

"Just taking a walk," Jenny said. "It's a beautiful day, isn't it?"

"Sure is," Kevin, the mailman nodded. "Are you planning to visit Jimmy?"

He looked back at the lighthouse.

"Not particularly," Heather wrinkled her nose.

Jenny said nothing.

"He's up and about today," Kevin told them. "A bit grumpy though."

"When is he not grumpy?" Heather asked.

"Stop by later at the café, Kevin," Jenny said. "I'll save a cupcake for you. It's a new recipe I am trying out."

"Can't say no to your cooking, Jenny," Kevin smiled. "See ya later."

"Looks like you don't like this

Jimmy," Jenny said to Heather as they saw Kevin reach the road and go out of sight.

"He's not really Mr. Sunshine. You'll see for yourself."

Jenny noticed the small cottage near the base of the lighthouse as they got closer. It was more like a shack or lean-to with a small porch and two rickety steps leading up to it. A tall, skinny man came out and sat down on the steps, digging his feet into the sand. He was bald and barefoot. A scraggly beard covered his chin and Jenny shrank back as the wind carried over an unpleasant smell. Stale liquor, sweat and who knows what else, Jenny decided.

"Howdy ladies!" the man hailed them.

"Looks like he's in a talking mood," Heather said under her breath.

She walked over and introduced Jenny.

"You that chicken necker everyone's been talking about?"

Jimmy Parsons spoke the dialect of the islanders. It was really strong in some people like Betty Sue and Eddie Cotton, people who had lived on the island all their lives.

"Be nice, Jimmy!" Heather warned.

Jimmy Parsons ignored her and continued talking to Jenny.

"Fellas say you make a mean sandwich."

"Why don't you come by the café sometime?" Jenny smiled. "I'll make my special chicken sandwich for you."

"Mighty kind of you," he nodded. "Say…what are you ladies doing out here at this hour?"

"Did you hear about the body they found a few days ago?" Jenny asked.

"What body?"

"A man died on this beach," Jenny explained. "Actually, he was murdered."

"How come I didn't know?" he asked.

"It was near the Newburys' beach," Heather supplied. "How far is that from here?"

"Not far," Jimmy said, scratching his beard. "Their property line starts a quarter of a mile down from here. You'll know when you see their warning sign."

"Have you seen this man before?" Jenny asked, whipping out the picture she carried everywhere.

Jimmy glanced at the photo briefly.

"Can't say I have. Is this the dead

guy? What was he doing out here?"

"That's what we are trying to find out," Jenny said grimly.

"Shouldn't the police be doing that?" Jimmy asked.

"They should..."

"Star was arrested," Heather spoke up suddenly. "Jenny's trying to prove she's innocent."

Jimmy's face changed color when he heard Star's name.

"What's Star got to do with it? Are the police daft? Go talk to that Hopkins boy."

"He's the one who arrested my

aunt," Jenny informed Jimmy.

He clutched his head suddenly and groaned. He stood up and went inside. Jenny and Heather looked at each other, wondering if he was coming back.

Jimmy Parsons came out, taking a swig from an amber colored bottle.

"What are ya'll yapping about? How does your aunt come into this, missy?"

"Star is Jenny's aunt," Heather bristled. "I thought you knew that."

Jimmy's eyes widened and he stared at Jenny.

"Say, are you that little girl that used to visit her 30 some years ago? You've puffed up quite a bit, huh?"

"I'm older now," Jenny blushed. "In my 40s."

"Show me that photo again," Jimmy demanded.

"Nothing comes to mind," he said, shaking his head again. "But I've been on the sauce too long. My brain's fried. I don't remember the last time I had a shower."

Jenny wanted to tell him it hadn't been any time recent.

"Will you let us know if you think about something?" Heather prompted.

"Sure! Anything for Star."

The girls said goodbye to Jimmy Parsons and walked on. Heather pointed to a 'No Trespassing' sign that was half buried in the sand.

"That must be the sign Grandma told us about."

Jenny stopped and turned to look around. The ocean occupied half her line of vision. The rest of it was a deserted beach. Any chances of someone having seen the dead man looked slim to her.

"Don't forget there were a lot of people here that day," Heather reminded her. "There were the party guests, and people who brought their own picnic."

"So he was a face in the crowd, you mean?" Jenny asked.

"He could have been a tourist who just stopped to look at the ocean, saw a crowd and wandered around to see what was going on."

"Why did someone kill him then?" Jenny asked. "There had to be a motive."

"Maybe someone followed him here, saw a chance and bashed his head in?"

"And nobody saw this?" Jenny asked.

"He could have been dead before the party started," Heather said. "Maybe he was just lying on the beach and people thought he's getting some sun."

"Surely it wasn't warm enough for that?"

"Tourists do strange things," Heather shrugged. "Locals have stopped paying attention to them."

A rambling house came into view and Jenny realized they had almost reached the Newburys' backyard.

"Maybe we should head back," she said, grabbing Heather's arm.

They had already been spotted. A uniformed maid came out on the patio and hailed them. Jenny and Heather waited until she came up to them. Jenny dreamed of a cool, frosty glass of lemonade. Surely the Newburys would offer them a drink?

"You are trespassing," the maid said as soon as she came closer. "This is the Newbury estate. It is private property."

The maid sounded as snooty as the woman who employed her.

"We were just walking on the beach," Heather stuttered. "We didn't realize this is your property."

The maid grimaced, making it clear what she thought of that.

"Isn't this where they found the dead man?" Jenny asked.

"I knew it!" the maid said triumphantly. "Tourists, or reporters?" she demanded.

"Tourists," Jenny said, looking apologetic.

"I had you pegged the moment I saw you," the young girl said.

Jenny leaned closer to the girl and whispered, "So? Show us where they found him."

The girl looked over her shoulder.

"I could get in trouble for this, you know."

"We won't tell anyone," Heather promised.

The girl walked a few steps away

from the house and stopped at a patch of grass.

"Somewhere around there, I think," she pointed with her finger. "At least that's where the police tape was. They took it off a few days ago."

"Do you know why?" Jenny asked.

The maid shrugged.

"They already caught the killer. Some old hippie woman from town, people say. Killed him with a paintbrush."

Chapter 10

Jenny had walked around the patch of grass the maid pointed out, looking for something unusual. She found nothing other than sand. She told Star about her visit to the beach and her strange encounter with Jimmy Parsons.

"Good old Jimmy," Star said.

"I gathered he's a good-for-nothing drunk."

"He wasn't always like that," Star said defensively.

"He knew nothing about the dead man," Jenny said. "But then he said he didn't remember anything so I don't know what to believe."

"Did he talk to the cops?"

"Apparently not. I don't know why the police haven't talked to him yet. I'm going to find out."

Jenny walked over to the police station the next day looking for Adam.

"He's in a bad mood," Nora warned. "His leg's acting up."

Jenny knocked and ignored Adam's command to leave him alone.

"Get out, Miss King," he growled. "Can't you see I'm busy?"

"This won't take long," Jenny said, ignoring his outburst.

She pulled out a chair and sat down in front of him.

"Have you talked to Jimmy Parsons?" she asked.

"What?"

"You know Jimmy Parsons, don't you? That old drunk who lives in the lighthouse?"

"I know who he is," Adam said, chewing on his lip. "What do you have against him, Jenny?"

"I ran into him yesterday and it appears he doesn't know anything about the dead guy."

Adam shrugged.

"Guy's stoned most of the time."

215

Jenny crossed her arms and glared at Adam.

"Why haven't the police interrogated him yet?"

Adam's eyes hardened.

"Are you going to tell me how to do my job?"

"I have to, since you're doing nothing. Jimmy Parsons might have been around when the guy was killed. But you would never know since you haven't even talked to him yet."

"When are you going to stop meddling, Jenny?" Adam asked coldly.

"I'm just trying to help!"

"Thank you for your suggestion. I'll think about it."

"Is that all?"

"That's all I can tell you at the moment."

Jenny stormed out of Adam's office and crossed the road. She was going to tackle Jason Stone next. It looked like incompetence ran high among the handsome men of Pelican Cove.

"Any progress?" Jenny barked as she barged into Jason's office.

Jason Stone was on the phone. He held up a finger, asking Jenny to give him a minute.

"Have a seat, Jenny," he said as

217

he hung up. "And calm down.
You're about to blow a gasket."

"The cops haven't talked to Jimmy
Parsons," Jenny fumed. "Can you
believe it?"

"Do you know that for a fact?"
Jason asked calmly.

"Jimmy said so!"

"Jimmy doesn't remember his
own name most days," Jason
dismissed. "I would take anything
he says with a pinch of salt."

"So he lied to me?" Jenny asked.

"He may have," Jason said. "But
I'm sure it wasn't deliberate."

Jason stood up and pulled out a

bottle of water from a small refrigerator in the corner. He handed it to Jenny.

"You need to keep your cool. We have a long way to go yet."

"I feel so helpless," Jenny said after she took a long gulp from the bottle. "We are no closer to exonerating Star."

"You need to take a break," Jason said.

He hesitated before he spoke again.

"Would you like to have dinner with me? They do a good surf and turf at the steakhouse."

"You're asking me out?" Jenny

frowned. "Frankly, Jason, I'm not in the mood to socialize. And I'm not divorced yet. Just separated."

"It's just dinner," Jason blushed. "I thought a change of scene would cheer you up."

Jenny allowed herself to sit back and breathe. What was she thinking? A smart, attractive man wanted to treat her to a fancy meal and she was lashing out at him?

"Dinner does sound nice, Jason," she said softly. "Thank you."

"Shall I pick you up then?" Jason brightened.

"Let's meet there at 7 PM."

Jenny walked back to the Boardwalk Café in a daze.

"Jason is taking me to dinner," she told Petunia as she poached chicken.

"Do you have a nice frock?" Petunia asked. "Go home early and take some time to get ready."

"It's not a date," Jenny started saying.

She stopped and smiled to herself. Maybe it was. She had gone through a rollercoaster of emotions since her husband dumped her. She was still dealing with a lot of anger and grief but she knew she was the victim. Any feelings she may have had for her husband had evaporated the day he drove her out and kept Cookie from her.

Jenny felt her excitement ramp up as the day passed. She left the café at 4 PM and took a long bath. Star wasn't around. There was a note telling Jenny she was working late at her gallery. Star often did that when she was working on a deadline for a special commission. Jenny was glad she hadn't burnt all her city clothes. She pulled out her trusty little black dress and wondered if it was too dressy. She decided to pair it with a string of coral beads and matching earrings. That made the outfit look just right.

Jenny walked over to the

Steakhouse, feeling a bit conscious. She ran into Captain Charlie just outside. He gave her a wink.

"Hot date?"

Jenny blushed.

"Just delivered the catch of the day," Captain Charlie nodded. "The Steakhouse has the best of everything. You're in for a treat."

He held up the bag he was carrying.

"The chef in there always has something for me."

Jenny spoke with Captain Charlie for a while and hurried inside. She didn't want to run into any more people she knew.

It was a few minutes to 7 PM but Jason Stone was already inside. Jenny liked a man who didn't keep her waiting. She tried not to think of all those dinner dates when her husband had turned up an hour late. Sometimes he hadn't turned up at all. Had she been too naïve and missed reading the signs? Jenny shook her head and decided she had to stop dwelling on the past.

Jason stood with his hands in his pockets and grinned at her. Jenny was glad to see he was wearing a sports jacket and leather shoes. She didn't feel overdressed.

"Hello, pretty lady!" Jason greeted

her, offering a fist bump.

She suddenly thought of her son Nick and his friends. So Jason was young at heart. That wasn't a bad thing.

"Have you tried our local wine yet?" Jason asked, playing the perfect host.

They opted for a merlot to go with their steak. Jenny tasted two different wines and chose the local vintage. Jason gave her an approving smile.

"So you really don't remember our first date, do you?" he asked as they waited for their crab cakes. "You ordered blueberry ice cream at the creamery and spilled it down your white shirt."

"I bet you mopped it up," Jenny said, then bit her lip.

She hadn't meant to sound crude.

"No such luck," Jason gave an exaggerated sigh. "Your aunt was watching us from the other end of the room. She came over and did the honors."

"I brought my aunt with me on a date?" Jenny laughed. "How do I not remember this?"

"You were barely 14, and super cute."

Jenny took a sip of wine and avoided saying anything. Jason's eyes darkened as he leaned forward.

"You still are, Jenny."

Their food arrived and Jason devoted his attention to it. He made sure Jenny liked everything and had what she wanted. Jenny tapped her spoon on the hard crust of her crème brulee.

"Is this where you bring all your first dates?"

"This is just dinner, remember?" Jason parried.

"I thought the Steakhouse was reserved for special occasions."

"This is a special occasion," Jason said quickly. "You are special, Jenny. I know you are used to

227

fancy clubs and restaurants. We don't have what the city offers..."

"And that's a good thing," Jenny assured him, rubbing one of the charms on her chain. "I had a great time tonight."

"I couldn't ask for more."

Jenny's phone rang and her heart skipped a beat. She wondered if her son was in trouble. Very few people had her cell phone number. She hardly used her phone since she came to Pelican Cove.

"I have to get this," she apologized. "It might be my son."

"Go ahead," Jason told her.

It was Star.

"Jenny, come quick! The cops are here."

"What? Where? Slow down, Auntie, and tell me what's happening."

She listened to Star's outburst for a few minutes and hung up.

"We have to go," she said, standing up. "That was Star. The police are at her gallery right now."

Jason didn't miss a beat. He handed over his credit card to the server and told her he would collect it later.

"Let's go, Jenny."

229

Jason drove his late model sedan to Star's art gallery. It took them less than five minutes to get there, barely enough time for Jenny to admire the soft leather seats and swanky sound system in the luxury car.

Star was standing outside, looking stricken. A paper fluttered in her hand. She handed it over to Jason.

"They gave me this...said they had a right to search the place."

Jason skimmed the document and looked at Jenny grimly.

"It's a warrant to search the art gallery. I'm afraid they also have one to search your house. Star's house, that is."

"What can we do now?"

"It's best to let them carry on," Jason advised. "We have nothing to hide. They might drop the charges against Star if they find nothing."

"That's good, right?" Jenny turned to Star. "That's what we want."

"They are trashing the place," Star said, "throwing canvases around."

The cops wanted to search Star's house after that. Jason drove the women home. They huddled outside on Star's porch while the police did their job.

"This is all so meaningless," Jenny cried. "Clearly, they are picking on Star because they don't have any other suspects. They are just putting on a show."

Jason hesitated before he spoke up.

"I hear the Newburys are putting the squeeze on. They want someone nailed for this as soon as possible."

"What do they care?"

"Ada Newbury is taking this murder as a personal affront. She wants to know who dared to kill the man on her property. She's vowed to drive that person out of Pelican Cove."

Jenny raised her eyebrows and curled her fingers into a fist.

"How do we know the Newburys didn't kill this man? He was found on their beach, right? They should be the top suspects."

"No one will dare point a finger at them in Pelican Cove," Jason said.

"But people do speak behind their back," Star argued. "We all know the Newburys aren't as above board as they claim to be."

"What does that mean?" Jenny demanded.

"Nothing!" Jason sighed. "Those are just rumors, Star. Throwing mud at the Newburys isn't going to help our case."

233

"I need to go talk to them," Jenny said with purpose. "Ada Newbury and her staff might have seen or heard something."

Jason coughed delicately.

"I don't think old Ada will give you the time of day, Jenny. She barely talks to your aunt."

"She can't say no to Betty Sue," Star spoke up.

"That's a good idea," Jason agreed. "Even Ada Newbury cannot say no to Betty Sue Morse."

"Look, I don't understand island politics," Jenny said, putting her hands on her hips. "But if Betty Sue can open that door for me,

I'll take her along. No big deal."

"Good luck with that," Jason said cryptically. "Those two have a volatile relationship. Betty Sue might just refuse to go with you."

"We'll see about that."

Chapter 11

"I don't see why you need me there," Betty Sue Morse protested.

She avoided looking at Jenny, her eyes trained on her needles as they pulled off an intricate stitch. Her knitting bag contained three skeins of wool that day, Easter colors of lavender, yellow and pink.

"You know why, Betty Sue," Petunia said as she walked onto the deck with a fresh pot of coffee.

"The police have already searched your aunt's place, Jenny," Molly spoke up. "And they didn't find anything. I think they will leave her alone now."

"They haven't dropped the charges against her. I'm sure the Newburys or their staff must have seen something."

"Didn't you talk to one of their maids?" Betty Sue asked.

"Heather says they have at least six maids," Jenny said stoutly.

"You're daft if you think Ada is going to let you talk to them," Betty Sue declared.

Her hands moved in a rhythm, twirling the different colors of wool around her knitting needles.

"You just get me in there," Jenny

said.

"There's no way the Newburys will let her in on her own," Heather said. "She needs you, Grandma."

Betty Sue pursed her mouth and looked at Petunia. Petunia's brow cleared.

"Oh! Is that why you are dawdling over going there, Betty Sue? Pay no heed."

"I'll be with you, Grandma," Heather assured her.

"What's going on?" Jenny asked, trying to understand the undercurrents.

"I will go with you," Betty Sue said. "But I am telling you this is a waste of time."

"You're going to rub Ada Newbury the wrong way, and then she'll make sure you repent," Molly told Jenny. "Don't say I didn't warn you."

Jenny stood up to leave but Heather sat her down.

"We can't just show up there. We have to get an appointment first."

Betty Sue used the phone in the café kitchen to call Ada Newbury. She didn't mince words. She had a frown on her face when she hung up.

"We are going there for tea tomorrow."

"Did you tell her I was coming with you?" Jenny asked.

"Don't be silly, girl. You are going to be an uninvited guest."

Jenny went about her chores at the café and spent a quiet evening at home. Star was at the gallery, busy putting it to rights after the police let her in. Jenny stepped out for a walk after a simple dinner of grilled fish and salad.

Tank came bounding up to her and held up his paw. He had stopped cowering when he met her. Jenny thought that was a good sign. Either his condition was improving or he had stopped thinking of her as a threat.

Two tall girls came running, calling out Tank's name. His tail wagged as he ran back to them. The girls were a mirror image of each other. Two pairs of cobalt blue eyes stared back at Jenny and smiled.

"Looks like he knows you," one of them said. "He's a bit wary of strangers."

"Tank and I are friends," Jenny nodded.

Jenny craned her neck and saw Adam limping up behind the girls.

"Hello Jenny! Have you met the twins?"

"Are these your girls?" Jenny asked, astounded.

None of her friends had mentioned Adam's kids before.

"They are so precious."

She turned and looked at them.

"Do you live here in town? How come I haven't seen you before?"

"Not anymore," one of the girls said, "although this is our home. We are at college now, in Charlottesville."

"We go to the University of Virginia," the other one said. "It's just four hours by road."

"Not close enough," Adam grumbled. "They are here to spend some time with their old man."

"Is it Spring Break already?" Jenny asked.

She had hoped her son Nick would come visit her during his break.

"Not yet," one of the twins said. "But we're going to Cancun for Spring Break. We thought we would come visit Dad before that."

Jenny invited them all in for a drink.

"Thanks Jenny," Adam said. "But we've got a tub of popcorn and a movie waiting for us at home. Maybe some other time."

"I have a son about your age," Jenny told the girls. "You should meet him when he visits."

"We'll spend some time here in the summer," the twins said.

Jenny walked on until she began feeling drowsy. She hoped the next day would provide some new information.

Betty Sue Morse reclined in the back seat of Jenny's car, holding Tootsie in her lap. She stroked Tootsie's fur and spoke to her in a soft voice.

"Will Ada be fine with Tootsie?" Jenny asked worriedly.

Ada Newbury seemed to have a problem with everyone.

"Tootsie seems a bit depressed

today," Betty Sue said. "How could I leave her on her own?"

"Ada likes Tootsie," Heather assured Jenny. "She was born on the Newbury estate. Ada was devoted to her mother."

"So Tootsie has a better pedigree than I do," Jenny said with a laugh.

Heather let out a snort that turned into full blown laughter.

"You never mentioned Adam Hopkins has kids?" Jenny asked Heather. "I ran into the twins last night."

"Just the twins?" Betty Sue asked.

"Adam was with them," Jenny

245

admitted.

"You're calling him Adam now, are you?" Betty Sue teased.

"His wife passed a few years ago," Heather said. "Adam raised the girls on his own since then. They are in college now."

"They are pretty," Jenny said.

"Not as pretty as their mother," Betty Sue said from the back seat. "She was beautiful. Adam's had a hard time, what with his war wounds and losing his wife."

"He seems tough," Jenny said.

"All the Survivors are tough. His ancestors came off the 'Bella, didn't they?"

"The 'Bella is the ship that sank in these parts, right?" Jenny asked. "I know a bit about it."

The road had curved up as they neared the Newbury estate.

"We're almost there," Betty Sue said, leaning forward. "Let me do the talking."

Betty Sue spoke imperiously to the security guard at the gates. He frowned at Jenny but let them in.

"I didn't know you were bringing guests," Ada said when she entered the parlor the maid had shown them into.

Tootsie looked up when she heard Ada's voice. Ada Newbury's face broke into a smile when she spotted the black poodle.

"Look who's here, Julius. Come here, Toots. Come give us a kiss."

Tootsie jumped down from Betty Sue's lap and ran to Ada. She scooped her up and allowed her to lick her face. Ada plopped down in a chair, holding Tootsie in her arms.

The little poodle's presence had softened her up. Jenny crossed her fingers and hoped her good mood would continue.

Julius Newbury entered the room and sat in a chair next to Ada. He was his usual cheery self. He greeted the ladies and offered them tea. A maid brought out a tea service with tiny cucumber sandwiches and cakes.

"Not as good as yours, I'm afraid," Julius said to Jenny. He leaned toward her and whispered dramatically. "Don't tell our cook I said that."

Jenny let the older man speak, biding her time. After ten minutes of inconsequential chatter, she decided to take the plunge.

"Have you recovered from the shock, Mr. Newbury?"

"What was that?" Ada raised her voice.

"The shock of having a man murdered in your home, of

course," Jenny said.

"My dear, we don't talk about such indelicate matters at tea," Ada pronounced with a sniff. "And that man was found somewhere on the beach, not in our home as you put it."

"But we heard he was found on your property," Jenny said, acting ignorant.

"You're right," Julius said. "We own a large parcel of land here. Most of the beach around here belongs to us."

"Julius!" Ada hissed.

Her gaze hardened as she looked at Jenny.

"Why are you here, Miss King?"

"We needed a ride," Betty Sue spoke up, "and Jenny wanted some feedback from you about the party. So we brought her along."

"I'm sorry to disappoint you, but I hardly tasted any of your confections," Ada said, sounding anything but sorry.

"I did," Julius said, ignoring his wife's glare. "And they were all lip smacking. Delicious!"

He kissed his fingers and made a smacking sound as he said that.

"Can I count on your recommendation?" Jenny asked eagerly.

"Absolutely!" Julius said.

Ada Newbury wasn't looking too pleased.

"Did you know that man?" Jenny asked. "The police still don't know his name."

"There were plenty of people on our beach that day," Ada dismissed.

Jenny pulled out the picture she carried everywhere.

"Why don't you just take a peep? Maybe you have seen him somewhere?"

Julius Newbury glanced at the picture and shook his head.

"Take that away," Ada ordered. "And stop talking about that incident."

"You mean the murder, don't you?" Jenny said. "This man practically died on your doorstep. Aren't you even a little bit curious about who he was or why he was here?"

Ada's ears turned red. She was beginning to look apoplectic.

Heather stood up and pulled Jenny to her feet.

"Jenny needs to visit the powder room. Come, Jenny, I'll take you there."

"But..."

253

"Just go," Betty Sue hissed.

Heather rushed out of the room with Jenny and paused in the foyer.

"Do you want to get us thrown out of here?" she panted.

She walked down another hallway and entered a room at the end.

A wizened old woman looked up and smiled when she saw them. She wore a chef's hat and a white apron covered her ample midsection. She was stirring some pots on the stove. A couple of uniformed maids chopped vegetables at a center island.

"Heather!" the woman said, holding out her arms. "You're a

sight for sore eyes."

"How are you, Cook?" Heather said, hugging her back.

"This is Jenny," she said, turning toward her friend. "She wants to ask you something about that man they found."

Cook made the sign of the cross.

"Don't let Madam hear you. We have been forbidden to talk about it."

Jenny almost shoved the man's picture in Cook's face.

"Please. Have you seen this man before?"

Cook looked at the picture for a

minute and shook her head.

"Can't say I have."

She handed it over to the two girls prepping the food.

"How about you, girls?"

They looked over the picture eagerly but shook their heads.

"How many more people work here?" Jenny asked. "We already talked to one other person."

The door opened and another girl in a maid's uniform came in. They had not met her before.

"Come and take a look at this picture," Cook said to the new girl. "Have you seen him before?"

The girl rolled her eyes and barely glanced at the picture Jenny was holding out.

"No..." she said in a bored tone.

"Look again, girl," Cook said sharply. "No need to be sassy."

The girl picked up the picture again, opening her mouth to speak before she took a glance. Her eyes widened a bit and she brought the paper closer, going in for a second look. She wavered a moment, then made up her mind.

"I've seen this guy," she nodded.

"Where?" Jenny and Heather said together.

"He was here a few nights ago."

"On the beach?" Jenny asked.

The girl shook her head.

"He was in the parlor with the master. I served them myself."

"Are you sure?" Heather asked. "Take a closer look."

The girl squared her shoulders and folded her arms.

"I've looked twice, haven't I? It was him alright."

"What were they talking about?" Jenny asked.

"How would I know?" the girl asked belligerently. "You think I hide behind doors and eavesdrop?"

Jenny thanked the girl and the rest of the women in the kitchen.

"Let's go, Jenny," Heather urged. "We've been gone long enough."

Cook tapped Heather on the shoulder as they turned to leave.

"Have you met him yet?"

Chapter 12

Jenny took a sip from her cup of tea. It was tepid. She was sure Ada Newbury would not ask for a fresh pot.

She was back in the parlor, sitting next to Betty Sue on a chintz covered sofa. A bead of perspiration lined Betty Sue's upper lip and her breath sounded labored. Jenny looked around the room and wondered what had happened in their absence.

A tall, stout man sat in a chair, staring into the fireplace. His shock of white hair hinted at his advanced years, as did his craggy face. Jenny peered at him, trying to guess where he had come from.

"How are you, Grandpa Robert?" Heather asked, stooping down to hug the man.

His face broke into a smile as he looked at Heather.

"Doing good, munchkin," he said, hugging her back. "I didn't know you were coming for tea."

"Betty Sue's come with a posse," Ada said.

"Have you met Grandma?" Heather asked the old man.

She looked at Betty Sue inquiringly.

"She hasn't said much," the man

said. "Nothing new about that."

Betty Sue crushed the hem of her dress in her fingers and smiled hesitantly.

"You are looking well, Robert," she said.

"This is my friend Jenny," Heather told the old man, pointing toward Jenny. "She's new in town."

The man called Robert nodded at Jenny but didn't say anything. Jenny was itching to show him the picture of the dead man. Betty Sue nudged her before she could do anything.

"We have to leave," Betty Sue Morse said.

She struggled to her feet and swayed. Jenny sprang up and took her arm.

"Robert, Julius…see you later," Betty Sue said.

They walked out of the parlor, Tootsie trotting behind them.

"Why don't you send Tootsie for a sleepover?" Ada Newbury called out.

Heather promised they would fix a date.

Jenny helped Betty Sue get in the back seat. Her face was red as a ripe tomato. She pulled out a lace handkerchief from her bag and dabbed her face with it.

"Are you okay, Grandma?" Heather asked with a frown.

"This is why I didn't want to come," Betty Sue muttered.

"Did something happen?" Jenny asked, mystified. "What's wrong?"

"Get in and start driving," Betty Sue ordered. "I want to get away from here as soon as possible."

Heather bit her lip and tried to hide a smile. No one spoke on the way back to town. Jenny pulled up outside the Boardwalk Café and they went in.

"You're back!" Petunia exclaimed when she saw them. "How was it?"

"Robert was there," Betty Sue hissed.

Jenny led them out on the deck and they sat at their favorite table, taking in the view of the boardwalk and the beach. The tide was coming in and Jenny let herself relax, smiling as the frothy waves battered the beach and receded with force.

"Are you feeling better now, Grandma?" Heather asked gently.

Petunia came out with a tray loaded with a fresh pot of coffee and some cupcakes. She set it down and sat next to Betty Sue, patting her on the back.

"Have a cupcake," she said

knowingly. "You'll feel better."

"Who was that man?" Jenny asked. "And why did you call him Grandpa, Heather?"

"He is my grandfather," Heather said softly.

She tipped her head toward Betty Sue.

"I don't understand," Jenny said densely. "Is he a relative? Why is he visiting the Newburys?"

Betty Sue expelled a big breath and closed her eyes.

"Robert is my husband, Jenny. Robert Newbury."

Jenny remembered her aunt

telling her how Betty Sue had kept her name after marriage.

"So you married a Newbury? I didn't know that."

"Julius is Robert's younger brother," Betty Sue said. "Robert and I stopped living together years ago."

Jenny didn't dare ask why.

"Grandpa Robert is my father's father," Heather elaborated.

"So you're actually a Newbury..." Jenny said, connecting the dots.

"She has Morse blood," Betty Sue said. "And Newbury blood too, I guess."

267

"Grandma still gets hot and bothered every time she sees her husband," Heather teased.

"Hush, girl," Betty Sue chided. "We should get going. There's a couple checking in this evening."

"Wait a minute," Jenny called out. "Don't you want to talk about what we found out, Heather?"

"Oh yes, I almost forgot."

Heather looked at Betty Sue and Petunia.

"They are doing it again."

"What have they done now?" Betty Sue asked grimly.

"One of the maids said the dead

man was having drinks with Julius."

Jenny was feeling left out. She hastened to explain.

"I showed him the picture, Petunia. He looked at it, really looked at it. But he said nothing."

"He lied to us," Heather said unnecessarily.

"Looks like they are up to their old tricks," Betty Sue smiled mirthlessly.

"You should stay out of this, Jenny," Petunia said. "The Newburys are powerful people. Who knows how or why they knew that man."

"But they must know who he is," Jenny cried. "Isn't that what we want to find out?"

"Leave it to the cops," Heather said.

"Are you protecting them because they are your relatives?" Jenny asked.

"Ada Newbury is no relation of mine," Betty Sue said. "But you don't know how evil she can be, girl. Don't get into their business."

Betty Sue and Heather left after that, leaving Jenny gaping after them.

"Have you heard from my aunt today?" she asked Petunia.

"Star's gone to the seafood market," Petunia told her. "She will stop here on her way back."

"Do you think the Newburys are involved in the murder?" Jenny asked her.

"They are not criminals, Jenny. Well, not exactly. Julius could be lying to hide something silly. Or he's just following Ada's orders."

"Why wouldn't they own up to knowing that man?"

"To avoid scandal, of course," Petunia said.

"That sounds silly," Jenny said angrily. "If the maid saw him in the house, I am sure someone else must have seen him too.

271

What about the security guy at the gate?"

"You could be right," Petunia said meekly. "But you won't get a word out of any of them. They won't dare go against Ada's orders."

"What about the police though? Surely they can't lie to the police?"

"Why don't you talk to the sheriff about this?" Petunia asked, a gleam lighting up her eyes. "Tomorrow morning sounds good. I hear he's left for the day."

"How would you know that?" Jenny sighed.

"He came here to grab a

sandwich," Petunia said. "Told me he had a doctor's appointment at 4 PM. It's way past that now."

Jenny spied Star coming up the steps of the café. She held up a bag.

"Got some fresh rockfish for us, sweetie. You ready to go home?"

Jenny was glad to see Star looking a bit upbeat. She had been moping ever since the police had ransacked her gallery.

"Can I help you prep something for tomorrow?" Jenny asked Petunia.

"It's all under control," the older woman assured her. "Why don't you go on home? I'll see you

273

tomorrow at six, bright and
early."

Jenny felt exhausted all of a
sudden. She was glad she wasn't
walking home. Captain Charlie
called out to them as they were
getting in the car.

"Had your chicken sandwich for
lunch, Jenny," he said, smacking
his lips. "I can't wait to get
another one tomorrow."

"I think I finally found
something," Jenny told her aunt
as she drove slowly across town.

The mail van crossed them and
Kevin gave them his usual salute.

Jenny told her aunt about her visit
to the Newbury estate.

"Betty Sue still cares about Robert," Star said, "even though they stopped living together a long time ago."

"Is that why she told me to forget about the Newburys?"

"Robert wasn't here on the day of Ada's Spring Gala. I doubt he is involved in all this."

Jenny decided she definitely needed to see the sheriff.

Star boiled potatoes and steamed broccoli while Jenny seasoned the fish with some lemon pepper. She wrapped it in foil with olive oil and slid it in the oven. Fifteen minutes later, they sat down to their healthy dinner.

"Do you miss him?" Star asked suddenly. "You were together for almost twenty years."

Jenny was quiet as she speared a piece of fish on her fork.

"I miss my old life. My routine. Shopping, making dinner, taking care of the house. Most days, I was asleep by the time he got home. I planned fancy dinners, then threw them out the next day."

"You are holding up pretty well, Jenny," Star said, "considering. I'm proud of you."

"I miss Nick," Jenny said softly. "I hope he comes to visit soon."

"He better spend some time with

us this summer," Star said. "I'll talk to him."

Jenny did the dishes after she convinced Star to go watch some TV. She gave everything a final rub down. She debated skipping her walk. Then she thought of the pancakes she had devoured at breakfast and strengthened her resolve.

The scent of roses and honeysuckle blended with the salty sea air and Jenny breathed it in deeply. Her mind was blessedly devoid of thought as she walked on the firm sand, letting the rhythmic sound of the ocean soothe her.

A tall figure appeared in the

distance and she felt her heart speed up. Tank bumped his head against her knee and put his paws on her chest, giving her a lick.

"You naughty boy," she laughed. "You're getting bolder by the day."

"He really likes you," Adam said. "And he's not afraid of you anymore."

"I like him too," Jenny said, taking Tank's head in her hands and hugging him close.

She pulled a ball out of her pocket and threw it in the distance. Tank ran after it, barking happily.

"How are you, Jenny?" Adam asked. "I came by the café earlier today. Petunia said you were out on an errand."

Jenny nodded, trying to decide if she should tackle Adam right away or wait until the next day. She couldn't hold herself back.

"I went to the Newbury estate with Betty Sue."

"Planning another party?" Adam asked mildly.

"They are hiding something, Adam!" Jenny burst out.

Adam flexed his shoulders as his eyebrows drew together in a frown.

"What have you done now, Jenny?"

"I haven't done anything," Jenny said, defending herself. "Have you questioned the Newburys yet? What about their staff?"

"That's part of an ongoing investigation," Adam said curtly. "I can't discuss it with you."

"That means you haven't. Looks like the Newburys have the police force in their pocket."

"That's a serious allegation, Jenny. I would think twice before I said anything."

"I have news for you, Mr. Sheriff," Jenny glowered, her hands on her hips. "The Newburys knew that dead man."

"What if they did?"

"If they are so innocent, why did Julius Newbury say he didn't recognize the man?"

"You showed him that sketch, did you?" Adam sighed. "The picture your aunt drew?"

Jenny didn't need to say anything.

"We have received some complaints," Adam continued. "People think you are harassing them."

"Who thinks that?" Jenny scoffed. "Not a single person I talked to said so."

"They won't say it to your face," Adam reasoned.

Jenny was speechless. Had she

281

been fooled by the friendly faces of the town people?

"I'm not too good at reading people," Jenny told Adam. "But I can guarantee none of the people I talked to felt harassed by my questions."

Adam shrugged. He'd had a hard day and he wasn't happy with the turn the conversation had taken.

"Whatever you say, Jenny," he said meekly. "Look, I am tired. I'll tell you the same thing I have been saying all along. Stop interfering in police work. Let us do our job."

"Are you ready to drop the charges against my aunt?"

Adam's gaze hardened and he shook his head in despair. He turned around and started walking away from Jenny.

Chapter 13

Jenny's phone rang early the next morning. It was 5:30 AM and she was in the shower, getting ready for her day. Star was asleep in her room. Her day started much later than Jenny's.

"Jenny, it's Petunia!" an excited voice burst out. "Come to the café immediately."

"What's the matter, Petunia? Are you alright?" Jenny asked, concerned.

"You just need to get here, girl."

"On my way," Jenny promised.

She pulled on a clean pair of jeans and the first sweater she got her hands on. She decided walking would be better than taking her car. Jenny set a brisk pace and she was turning on to Main Street fifteen minutes later, keeping an eye out for Petunia. It was ten minutes to six, her usual time to get to work.

Two patrol cars idled in front of the café. One of them had its lights on and the flashing beacons lit up the street in the delicate light of the morning. The sky was overcast and Jenny saw a sliver of the sun peeping through the clouds at the horizon.

She could see a bunch of people standing on the sidewalk, staring up at the café. Jenny's heart gave a leap. She suddenly felt afraid.

Had there been an accident in the café? Had anything happened to Petunia?

She picked up her pace and almost jogged the rest of the way. A figure on the sidewalk turned around and she came face to face with Captain Charlie. It was the first time Jenny had seen a frown on his face.

She bounded up the stairs and stopped in her tracks, her mouth hanging open in shock. Angry red graffiti greeted her at the entrance of the café. It covered every possible surface, the white washed café walls, the blue front door which was locked at night and the shingled roof.

"Get Out", screamed the words painted on one wall. Another one warned them to "Stop" and "Leave".

Jenny spotted Petunia sitting at a table in the corner. She was surrounded by some deputies. Adam stood before her, leaning heavily on his cane. His uniform was wrinkled, as if he had thrown on the previous day's one in haste. Tears streamed down Petunia's eyes and she had a lost look in them.

Jenny ran over and hugged the older woman.

"Oh my God, Petunia, what's going on?"

"Jenny! I am glad to see you, girl. Look what they did."

Jenny straightened and spared a second look at the destruction. She was beginning to get riled up.

"Who did this?" she demanded furiously, glaring at Adam. "What are you doing to catch the culprit?"

Adam had a resigned look.

"I first need to make sure nobody is hurt," he said.

He took Petunia's hand in his and said gently, "Do you want to tell me what happened?"

Petunia was sobbing silently, her chest heaving as she gulped in deep breaths between her sobs. She nodded her head and looked up at Adam.

"I couldn't sleep. I got ready and came here earlier than usual. I thought I would start the coffee and put in the first batch of muffins. The regulars start coming in at six anyway."

Adam nodded, encouraging her to go on.

"I saw someone scurry down the side when I turned onto Main Street. I wasn't really paying attention at the time."

"Did you recognize who it was?"

Petunia shook her head.

"Like I said, I wasn't really looking. I sat down on that bench for a few minutes to watch the sun come up." She paused and swallowed. "I like to do that, see? It's one of my favorite ways to start the day."

Adam didn't interrupt her.

"The sun wasn't coming up...I mean, I couldn't really see it due to the clouds. So I got up and walked to the café. I wasn't in a hurry. I had no idea what had gone down here."

"You called me around 5:30," Jenny reminded her.

"I came up the steps and saw all this!" Petunia wailed. "I opened the door, trying hard not to disturb anything. I called the police first. Then I called you, Jenny."

Jenny put her hands on Petunia's shoulders and squeezed them.

"You did the right thing. What are the police doing to help us?"

"The paint is still wet in some places," Adam said.

"Good. It will be easier to wash it off."

"Not so soon, Jenny. This is a crime scene now. We need to process it, take pictures, dust for fingerprints..."

"What about the morning rush?"

Petunia asked. "The watermen will be here for their coffee. Captain Charlie's already waiting on the sidewalk."

"I don't think you can open the café today, Petunia," Adam said firmly. "We need to get started here. We'll hand it over to you as soon as possible."

"What about cleanup?" Jenny asked.

"You can't do that until we're done here."

"Has this happened before?" Jenny asked Adam. "I thought this kind of vandalism was limited to the city."

Adam pursed his lips before he

spoke.

"I don't think this is vandalism. Have you read what it says?"

"Not really...I just saw something scrawled everywhere. Give me a minute."

Jenny walked around the deck, trying to absorb the scene of destruction. Something clicked in her mind. She whirled around to confront Adam.

"Am I the target here?"

"Sure looks like it, Jenny. The Boardwalk Café has been here for years and Petunia has been running it without incident for the last 25 years. You're the only thing that's new here."

"So someone wants to drive me out of Pelican Cove?"

Adam shrugged. "I can't say anything definite until we investigate further."

"You never say anything more than that!" Jenny snapped.

The crowd on the sidewalk had grown while Jenny was talking to Petunia. Heather pushed through the crowd and ran up the steps.

"Jenny? Petunia? Are you safe?"

Her hand rose to her mouth as she looked around at the scene.

"Who would do all this?"

Petunia clutched Heather's hand

and leaned against her.

"I'm glad to see you, dear."

"So am I," Heather said with a shake of her head. "I almost forgot. Grandma sent me here with a message. We figured they might shut the café down for some time. I pulled out our spare coffee maker and put in an extra batch of muffins at the inn. We can take care of all your regulars."

"That's a relief," Petunia said, giving Heather a watery smile. "People depend on us, you know. I can't send the men off on the water without their coffee."

"That's a good idea," Adam

295

approved. "Nice of you to come through, Heather."

He turned toward Jenny.

"Why don't you head on to the Bayview Inn? We are going to be busy here for a while."

"I have many more questions," Jenny argued.

"I'm sure you do," Adam soothed. "But they can wait. Let us do our job, Jenny, please. We can talk later."

Jenny didn't look pleased but she gave in. She took Petunia's arm and helped her up.

"I guess we are going to the Bayview Inn."

"Jenny!" someone called out faintly.

Jenny turned to see Star hurrying up the sidewalk. She was wearing a colorful dress but her hair was in disarray and her eyes were swollen with sleep.

"How's my Jenny?" Star cried as she rushed up the café steps. "Petunia? Where are you?"

Jenny engulfed her aunt in her arms and tried to calm her down.

"I'm fine, Auntie, I'm fine. No one has been hurt. It was just a prank."

Star looked around in fright, taking in the scene.

"This is more than a prank. What if you had walked in on them? You could have been hurt."

"But I wasn't and neither was Petunia," Jenny stressed.

Jenny forced her aunt to sit down and gave her a quick report.

"Let's go to the inn then," Star nodded. "I need some coffee in my system."

The crowd seemed mollified when they learned they were going to be served coffee at the inn. They waited for a few minutes and started following the women.

Jenny spent a busy morning working in an unfamiliar kitchen, trying not to bump into Heather.

Luckily, there weren't too many guests at the inn. They checked out after breakfast.

Petunia, Star and Betty Sue Morse sat at the small kitchen table, their heads together. Jenny had told Petunia to take it easy for a while and she hadn't argued.

"What have they got against my Jenny?" Star was saying. "I know she's new in town. But why would anyone want to drive her out?"

"I think I know why," Heather spoke up as she placed a plate of muffins before the ladies. "This is related to that dead man."

"What?" everyone exclaimed.

"Just think about it," Heather

reasoned. "Jenny has been going around town showing everyone that picture. She must have rattled someone."

"But nobody recognized that picture," Betty Sue said.

"That's what they said," Star told her. "But if someone in town did kill that man…"

"Someone has been lying to us," Petunia finished Star's sentence.

"You must be getting close, Jenny," Heather said. "That's why this person is trying to threaten you."

"I'm not going anywhere," Jenny said firmly.

"How many people did you show the picture to?" Petunia asked.

"Dozens," Jenny replied.

"It must be someone you talked to in the last day or two," Star reasoned.

"We went to the Newbury estate yesterday," Jenny said slowly. "We know they were lying to us."

"Do you think they found out that maid talked to us?" Heather asked.

"Ada will not stoop so low," Betty Sue said with conviction. "She might fire the maid, or give you the cold shoulder, Jenny, but she is not going to hire goons and trash the Boardwalk Café."

"We talked to Jimmy Parsons," Jenny reminded them. "He doesn't seem like a model citizen."

"He may be a drunk," Betty Sue objected. "But he is a Parsons. I don't think he would do this."

Jenny didn't agree with Betty Sue.

"If you ask me, this is exactly what a drunk would do. He is too afraid to confront us so he is stabbing us in the back."

"Maybe it's neither of them," Heather mused. "There's someone who we don't suspect yet but someone who knows what we're up to, someone who's watching us."

"That could be anyone in town," Petunia cried. "How can we protect ourselves against an unknown adversary?"

"That's it," Jenny said resolutely. "I must stop working at the café."

"What?" everyone cried.

"That won't solve anything," Petunia said grimly. "You will still be in town and you will be a target."

"At least they won't target you, Petunia," Jenny said. "I am so sorry for all this. I will pay for any damages."

"Honey, this is not your fault," Star said. "But I agree. Maybe you should stay away from the

Boardwalk Café for a few days."

"Jenny's not going anywhere," Petunia said stoutly. "I need her right beside me as soon as we reopen the café."

"That's nice of you, Petunia," Jenny said. "But what do we do next?"

"We soldier on," the older woman told Jenny. "And we keep showing that picture around. Sooner or later, someone will slip up and we will find something."

"Don't forget the police are working on this too," Heather reminded them.

"I have to go and talk to Adam," Jenny said, pulling off her apron.

"You do that, honey," Betty Sue Morse said, giving the other women a knowing look. "Go talk to that Hopkins boy."

Chapter 14

Jenny's meeting with Adam didn't produce any results. She accused him of not investigating enough and he told her to stay out of police business. It was as if any rapport they had built over their evening walks had evaporated.

"Be careful, Jenny," Adam called out as she stomped out of his office. "You have obviously ruffled some feathers."

"What do you think I should do?" she demanded. "Just lock myself in and sit at home? I have a café to run, Adam, and I am not going to let some coward dictate how I live my life."

"I know what you mean," Adam said. "Just be a bit vigilant. And if you see anything suspicious or come across any new face, let me know immediately."

"You think this is the work of an outsider?"

Adam didn't answer right away.

"This kind of thing has never happened in Pelican Cove. Most people here have known each other for generations. Do they have feuds or bear grudges? Sure. But no one has actually acted out on them."

"I guess you'll blame me for that too."

"Nobody's blaming you," Adam

sighed. "Just be careful, okay?"

Jenny gave him a barely perceptible nod and breezed out.

"Sorry to hear about the café," Nora at the front desk called out. "How's Petunia taking it?"

Jenny chatted with Nora for a while and stepped out of the police station. Her eyes fell upon Jason Stone's office. She hadn't talked to him after that incident at her aunt's gallery. She crossed the road and walked in, feeling a bit breathless. She told herself it was from all the walking around she had done in the past hour.

Jason jumped up from his chair as soon as he saw her.

"Jenny!" he cried, coming around his desk and grabbing her shoulders. "Are you alright?"

He gave her a once over and hugged her tight. Jenny tried not to blush.

"I'm okay, I'm okay," she protested, wriggling out of his embrace. "Neither Petunia nor I were there when that guy trashed the place."

"Don't make assumptions," Jason said immediately. "It could have been a woman. Spraying paint does not require a lot of upper body strength."

"You're right of course," Jenny said, having an aha moment. "I never thought of that."

"Come and sit down first," Jason said. "Can I get you something? Coffee? Something stronger?"

"I wish I could say yes to something stronger," Jenny smiled, "but it's barely noon."

"We have extenuating circumstances," Jason assured her. "So? What is it going to be?"

Jenny opted for a bottle of water from Jason. She gulped down half of it and sat there, her chest heaving as she tried to calm down.

"I never thanked you for dinner," she said.

"No thanks needed. I hope you weren't totally bored…"

"Just a wee bit…" Jenny joked. "But seriously, I had a good time, Jason. It's been a while since I enjoyed a nice dinner in a fancy restaurant."

"I'm sure you are used to fancier places," Jason smiled. "How about an encore, since we were interrupted the first time?"

Jenny gazed into his chocolate brown eyes. Milk chocolate, Jenny decided, or caramel. Once again Jenny was struck by how handsome Jason was with his finely sculpted looks. He probably owed it to some aristocratic British ancestor, she thought, remembering the Stones were one of the early settlers on the island.

"I'd like that," Jenny said shyly, coming out of her reverie.

"We can check out a place I know in Chincoteague," Jason said. "It's a few miles up north. We'll have a nice drive."

"I'm up for it," Jenny said wholeheartedly. "I need to get back to the inn now."

Adam had called the Bayview Inn in Jenny's absence. The police were done with the café.

"We have permission to open our doors," Petunia said. "But we have a big mess on our hands."

"Chris is coming around with some paint," Heather said, hanging up the inn phone. "We'll fix everything in no time, Petunia, don't you worry."

The ladies got to work and Chris just painted over the red paint. Jenny washed down the front deck and made sure everything was sparkling clean again. Thankfully, the interior of the café was intact. Jenny started working in the kitchen.

"I think we should take a breather today," Petunia decided. "We will open tomorrow morning as usual."

Jenny started walking home as the sun dipped close to the water.

The sky had cleared during the day and there was no sign of the clouds that lined the horizon that morning. She hummed a tune to herself as she walked along, lost in thought.

She cried out as she struck an immovable wall and rubbed her elbow. She looked up into the cloudy eyes of Jimmy Parsons. He swayed in front of her but then managed to gather himself.

"Look where you're going, missy," he growled.

"You watch your step, Mr. Parsons," Jenny shot back.

She felt her day catch up with her and suddenly felt very frail. She didn't have the energy to parry insults with anyone.

"You owe me a drink," Jimmy Parsons grumbled belligerently.

Jenny let out a snort and started walking past him. Jimmy held her arm in an iron grip.

"Didn't you hear me, girlie? Buy me a drink at the Rusty Anchor."

"Why would I do that?"

"You're a menace, that's why. You have caused trouble ever since you came to town."

"What did I do to you, Mr. Parsons?" Jenny demanded, her hands on her hips.

Her arm hurt from where Jimmy had grabbed it. Jenny reflected he had a lot of strength for someone who was on a liquid diet most of the time.

"That Hopkins boy came by with his people, didn't he? Woke me up from my nap. Asked all kinds of silly questions..."

"Oh yeah? Like what?"

"Wanted to know where I was at 5 AM this morning," Jimmy grumbled. "How am I supposed to know that?"

Jenny realized Jimmy Parsons was in a talkative mood. It was a good time to milk him for more information. She made up her mind.

"Let's go get that drink, Mr. Parsons."

Jimmy's face broke into a smile. He offered her his arm and swayed a bit on his heels. Jenny wasn't sure if it was a gallant gesture or a need for support but she took it.

Jimmy must have showered since the last time Jenny had seen him. He didn't smell as bad as she feared. His salt and pepper beard covered a small scar.

"Is that a birthmark?" Jenny asked.

"Never mind that," Jimmy said quickly.

They went into the Rusty Anchor and Eddie called out a greeting. His eyes held an unspoken question. Jenny grabbed a table close to the bar and sat down.

Jimmy ordered three beers for them.

"Is someone joining us?" Jenny asked.

Jimmy swallowed half of his in a single gulp and rubbed his mouth with the back of his hand.

"It's for me. I figure you must be a slow drinker."

Jenny nodded mutely. Her hands trembled as she picked up the beer mug. She felt a lot of eyes turn and stare at them and suddenly felt vulnerable.

"What are ya'll staring at?" Jimmy growled, looking around the bar.

Most people averted their eyes and looked away.

"So I hear there was some trouble at the Boardwalk Café today?" Jimmy said. "Is Star alright?"

"Why wouldn't Star be okay?" Jenny asked, surprised. "She was at home."

"She spends a lot of time there with that Clark woman."

"The café was closed. No one was hurt."

Jimmy nodded to himself. He had

drained both his beers. He called out for more, then stood up and waddled to the bar to pick it up.

Jenny's eyes fell on Jimmy's wallet. He had pulled it out of his pocket and put it on the table when he sat down. Jenny had a déjà vu moment. Her husband used to do that. Jenny leaned closer as she spied the logo of an expensive leather brand embossed in the wallet. She was about to touch it to make sure when Jimmy came back.

"You're not planning to pinch a fiver from me, are you?" he spoke.

"What? Of course not, Mr. Parsons. I was just admiring the

leather."

"Call me Jimmy," he invited. "We are friends now that we shared a pint."

Jimmy held two mugs of beer, one in each hand, and hesitated as if trying to decide which one he should drink from first. He drained the glass in his left hand and set it on the table with a bang.

Jenny opened and closed her mouth like a fish.

"Don't worry, you're not paying for these," Jimmy assured her. "You can just pay for the first one."

He picked up the wallet and pulled out some cash. He slapped them on the desk and put the empty beer mug on them. He stood up again and swayed on his feet.

"Be right back," he slurred.

Eddie came by with a tray and loaded the empty beer mugs. He counted the notes and put them on the tray.

"Didn't know you were hanging out with the town drunk, Jenny," he sniggered, slapping something down on the table.

Jenny picked up the piece of paper as soon as Eddie left. It was crumpled and yellow with age. She turned it over and her eyebrows shot up as a familiar face stared back at her. It was the man from Star's drawing. Jenny hastily put the paper in her bag and straightened up.

Jimmy came back a minute later and Jenny made her excuses.

"It was nice catching up with you, Jimmy," she said, trying to sound sincere. "I have to go now."

"Tell Star I said Hello," he said moodily and waved her off.

Jenny wondered how long he would sit there and how many more beers he would guzzle.

"You are sure this is the same guy?" Jenny asked Star as they sat in their living room after dinner. They had just finished dinner. Star had offered to cook and produced a simple dinner of pasta and store bought sauce. Jenny had been patient as she twirled the noodles on her fork and chewed on her garlic bread but her head had been working on all kinds of scenarios. She was sure of one thing. Jimmy Parsons was hiding something.

Star turned the picture over in her hands again.

"Jimmy's not a bad sort," she said. "I'm sure there must be an easy explanation."

"Like what?" Jenny asked. "You think he stole that man's wallet?"

Star looked at Jenny indignantly.

"What did I say about Jimmy? He

is not a thief, Jenny. He doesn't go around robbing tourists."

"The wallet was the kind my husband used to have. It costs a pretty penny. I am sure Jimmy didn't buy it."

"Someone could have given it to him," Star said. "Or he might have found it somewhere."

"Why didn't he tell us that?"

"He knows he's a pariah," Star stressed. "He doesn't talk much. I am surprised he talked to you today."

"I have a theory about that," Jenny said mildly.

She suspected Jimmy Parsons had

a soft spot for her aunt.

"I think you shouldn't worry about how Jimmy got this," Star repeated. "There has to be an easy explanation."

"Let's go with that," Jenny agreed. "What does this picture prove?"

"The man lost his wallet?" Star asked, shrugging her shoulders.

"I think we can safely say this man came to Pelican Cove for some reason. He was on the beach around Jimmy's lighthouse and he visited the Newburys. The question is, who else did he meet?"

Chapter 15

The line stretching outside the Boardwalk Café kept Jenny and Petunia on their feet the next day. People were curious about who had trashed the café and why.

"We are actually running out of coffee," Jenny said as she put on a fresh pot.

"Most people are here to gossip," Petunia noted.

"They keep drinking cup after cup of coffee without ordering anything else," Jenny grumbled.

"It's time we took a break," Petunia said weakly. "I can't wait to get home and soak my feet in a tub of water."

Betty Sue, Heather and Molly sat on the deck at their usual table, waiting for Jenny and Petunia to join them. Star came up the steps, holding a big canvas wrapped in cloth. She set it down against the café wall and sat down.

Betty Sue was knitting a snowy white scarf with a pink border. Molly had her head in a book. Heather was tapping her fingers on the scuffed wood table, staring impatiently at the sea.

"What's the matter?" Star asked her. "Thinking about Chris?"

Heather turned red but said nothing. Chris had asked her to dinner at the Steakhouse again.

Heather was trying to anticipate what he had planned for the night.

Jenny and Petunia finally came out.

"That's it," Petunia sighed. "I put a fresh pot of coffee out on the counter and told people they could help themselves. We need to catch our breath for a few minutes."

Jenny carried a plate piled high with sandwiches. She sat down and bit into one, too tired to say anything much.

"The town's buzzing," Betty Sue said to Jenny. "Everyone's talking about your date with Jimmy

Parsons."

"I just shared a drink with him," Jenny said with surprise.

"Most people here don't give him a second glance," Betty Sue said. "You know that, don't you?"

Jenny shrugged. She hadn't exactly thought about it.

"He's the town drunk for a reason," Betty Sue continued.

"Have I committed a social blunder then?" Jenny asked the women. "Done something unforgivable?"

Betty Sue Morse smiled at her.

"Jimmy's harmless. But he's too

old for you."

"I am not attracted to him or anything," Jenny laughed. "He asked me to buy him a drink and I went along. It was just a beer at the Rusty Anchor."

"Show them that photo," Star said.

Molly finally pulled her head out of her book.

"Are you still going around town with that picture, Jenny?"

"This is a different one," Jenny told them.

She turned to look at her aunt.

"I don't have it with me now."

"Tell us more," Heather said, looking interested.

"It's a picture of our dead guy," Jenny said. "It fell out of Jimmy Parson's wallet."

Betty Sue, Heather and Petunia stared at her with their mouths hanging open. Molly had a frown on her face.

"Here we go again," she said, rolling her eyes. "You're like a child with a new toy."

"You don't think this is significant?" Jenny asked her. "Wait till you hear this. That picture fell out of a shiny new leather wallet. I think that wallet belonged to that guy."

"Jimmy's not a thief," Betty Sue said firmly.

"That's what I told her," Star said.

"Let's say he didn't steal it," Jenny said, holding up her hand. "I'm willing to concede that. But he did find it somewhere. That means the man was definitely in town for some reason."

"How many people have you showed that picture to?" Heather asked. "You could have missed someone. There are people who don't come to the Boardwalk Café."

"Adam's already giving me grief about showing that picture around," Jenny said. "I can't knock on people's doors and ask them about it."

"It's up in the library, isn't it?" Betty Sue asked.

She turned to Molly.

"Did you put it up there like we told you to?"

Molly gave them an affirmative nod.

"Maybe he just sneaked around at night. He could have driven straight to the Newbury estate. He might have walked on the beach around there and dropped his wallet."

"Where do people go when the Bayview Inn is full?" Jenny asked.

Heather slapped her hand on the table.

"They go to a neighboring town of course. There's a chain motel five miles out of town and then there are other inns and bed and breakfasts up and down the coast. He could have been staying at any of those."

"Let's go and talk to some people in the neighboring towns then," Jenny said. "What do you say, Heather?"

"I say you have too much time on your hands," Molly said, getting up. "I have to get back to work. I am taking the scenic route back."

She walked down the café steps

that led to the boardwalk and started walking in the opposite direction.

"Have you noticed how she gets up and leaves every time we talk about that guy?" Petunia asked. "That girl is weird."

"I guess she really needs to get back to her desk," Jenny reasoned, taking her friend's side.

"Are you on social?" Heather asked Jenny. "We have an online group of the local hotel and inn owners. We post messages and ask for help in emergencies. They are a pretty helpful bunch. We all want to boost tourism in the area."

"How can they help?" Jenny asked.

"We can post that man's picture in the group and ask anyone if they recognize it," Heather said. "I should have thought of it before."

"Let's do that," Jenny agreed. "But I need to go get my laptop."

"Why don't you and Heather head on to Star's cottage?" Petunia said helpfully. "You can post the photo and come back here after that."

"I can help while Jenny's gone," Star offered. "I need to take some time off from my art today."

Jenny and Heather were back barely an hour later. They had

posted the photo in the group and asked people to call Jenny's phone if they had any information. Jenny's phone rang the minute she entered the café.

Her face lit up as she listened to the voice at the other end. She motioned Heather to wait. Jenny hung up a couple of minutes later.

"It was an inn in Cape Charles. Do you know where that is?"

"It's a few miles south on Route 13," Heather nodded. "What did they say?"

"A man fitting the description checked in at their inn. He said he had business in Pelican Cove. He checked out a few days ago."

"We need to go talk to them," Heather said eagerly. "Shall we go now?"

"Go!" Petunia said before Jenny had a chance to get her permission. "Come back with some news."

Jenny and Heather walked to Star's cottage again to pick up Jenny's car. They drove out of town and Jenny put in the address of the inn in her GPS. They were soon pulling up outside a quaint inn overlooking the Chesapeake Bay.

An old white haired lady greeted them at the door.

"Welcome to the Sunset Point

Inn," she said cheerily. "Come on in. I have fresh cookies."

Jenny opened her mouth to fire off her questions but Heather grabbed her arm and gave her a meaningful look. Jenny let the old woman lead them inside.

"I'm Victoria," the woman introduced herself. "Which one of you did I talk to on the phone?"

"That was me," Jenny said, holding out her hand. "I'm Jenny and this is Heather. She runs the Bayview Inn with her grandma."

"Oh, you're Betty Sue's child, aren't you?" the woman said.

Jenny silently tried to guess the woman's age. Her hair was snow white and glossy, tied neatly in a bun at the nape of her neck. She wore a printed floral dress with a white lace collar. The brooch pin at her throat contained a sparkling green stone that matched her eyes.

Victoria led them to a small parlor. Floral print sofas were placed around a coffee table. Rose patterned wallpaper covered the walls. A fluffy white cat sat in one of the chairs.

Jenny and Heather sipped the tea Victoria poured and ate some of the shortbread cookies. They were still warm from the oven.

Jenny finally looked at Heather for approval and fished out the man's picture from her bag.

"That's him alright," Victoria said. "I gave him our best room. We are not really full this time of the year."

"How long did he stay?" Jenny asked. "Do you know why he was here?"

"He was here for two nights," Victoria told them. "Said he had to meet someone in Pelican Cove."

"Why didn't he stay in town then?" Heather asked.

"He told me the local inn was full," Victoria shrugged. "I didn't probe any further."

"Did he say anything about what brought him here?"

Victoria shook her head.

"Our guests value their privacy. He paid cash in advance so I didn't ask too many questions."

"What about his address?" Heather asked.

"He was from the city," Victoria said, "somewhere near Washington DC. That's all I know."

"What about his name?" Jenny asked, barely able to hold back her excitement.

Victoria picked up a book from a rolltop desk that stood against a

343

wall. She rifled through the pages until she found what she was looking for.

"John Smith," she said with a smile.

Jenny's face fell.

"Are you sure?" she asked Victoria.

"That's what it says here," the woman said, suddenly looking her age.

"Did you cross check it against a photo ID?" Jenny pressed.

Victoria coughed into a lace handkerchief. She was beginning to look flustered. She shook her head.

"We don't do that here at the Sunset Point Inn," she said apologetically. "My Daddy believed in trusting his fellow men."

"Your Daddy was a wise man," Jenny said gently.

The girls bid farewell to Victoria and turned around to go back to Pelican Cove.

"That was a bust," Jenny sighed.

"You don't think his name is really John Smith?" Heather asked.

"What are the chances, Heather? You tell me."

"It's not impossible," Heather argued. "But I guess it is

345

improbable."

"I need to talk to Adam again," Jenny said firmly. "I think Jimmy may know more than he is letting on. Only Adam can make him talk."

Heather said nothing and stared out of the window.

"You're very quiet all of a sudden," Jenny said. "Had a fight with Chris?"

"Anything but..." Heather said bitterly.

"Do you *want* to have a fight with him?" Jenny asked, puzzled.

"We're going to the Steakhouse again," Heather asked. "That's as good as a commitment."

"Don't be silly," Jenny consoled. "Jason Stone took me to dinner at the Steakhouse. Does that mean we are 'seeing' each other?"

"You don't know this town, Jenny," Heather objected. "People already think we have an understanding because of our families. Going to the Steakhouse twice so close together will seal the deal in the eyes of the people."

"And you don't want that, I presume?" Jenny said, finally connecting the dots. "Do you not like Chris?"

"Chris is a great guy," Heather

said brightly.

"But...?"

"I'm not sure we have a future together," Heather admitted. "I like him. I more than like him. Any girl would be lucky to have him."

"But you are not that girl?"

Heather shrugged.

"I don't know, Jenny. I'm confused."

"Is there someone else?" Jenny asked, rolling her eyes as she turned onto the bridge that would take them to the island. Built in the 1970s, it had connected the island to the rest of the world.

Star had taken that very bridge when she arrived in Pelican Cove all those years ago.

Heather shook her head.

"Not exactly...not yet, at least."

"So you fancy someone else!" Jenny declared triumphantly. "Why didn't you say so?"

"It may be nothing," Heather said softly. "I do like Chris."

Jenny drove slowly through the town while the girls talked about Heather's love life. She reached Star's house a few minutes later.

Heather said goodbye and Jenny marched toward the police station. She had a bone to pick with Adam Hopkins.

Chapter 16

"What are you going to do about this John Smith?" Jenny asked Adam.

She had given him a detailed account of her trip to Cape Charles and their conversation with Victoria, the old inn keeper.

Adam looked thoughtful.

"As you say, this must be a fake name," he finally admitted.

Jenny was surprised to see him agreeing with her.

"It could be real too though," Adam added. "It's a common name because many people have that name."

"Forget about his name for a minute," Jenny said, pulling at her necklace and rolling a four leaf clover between her fingers. "What was Jimmy Parsons doing with that wallet?"

"He must have found it on the beach," Adam shrugged.

"Must have?" Jenny screamed. "Are you going to leave it at that?"

Adam's gaze hardened as he looked at Jenny.

"We will take the appropriate action, Madam."

"You are letting your personal feelings for the man cloud your judgment."

"What do you mean?" Adam asked with a frown. "What feelings?"

"I know you're part of a clique," Jenny scoffed. "Your families came from that sinking ship and so you have some kind of unbreakable bond. Is that why you're letting him run free?"

"Be very careful about what you say, Jenny," Adam spit out. "Don't go around making baseless accusations."

"Why won't you believe that Jimmy Parsons might have killed the guy?"

Adam balled his hands into a fist and banged it on the table.

"He has an alibi."

He banged his fist on the table again when Jenny opened her mouth to argue.

"It's iron clad, and I am not going to tell you what it is."

Jenny stood up and stormed out of the police station without saying goodbye to Nora.

She spent the day banging pots in the kitchen. Petunia didn't dare say anything to her. She was just glad Jenny wasn't out serving the customers.

"If Jimmy Parsons is innocent, we are at a dead end," Jenny exclaimed over dinner.

Star calmly cut a piece of oven baked barbecued chicken and looked at Jenny.

"Why are you so hung up on Jimmy being guilty?" she asked. "What's he done to you?"

"I have nothing against him personally," Jenny sighed. "But he's the only unsavory person we have come across so far."

"He's harmless, Jenny."

"He may be harmless, but I still don't believe he is free of blame. How did he get his hands on that wallet, Star?"

"Forget about the wallet," Star said. "Whoever murdered that guy is pretty clever. I'm beginning to think he got away with it."

"He or she," Jenny corrected her aunt. "And we can't have that. I need to clear my mind and start from the top."

Jenny walked around for what seemed like hours that night. She sat staring at the ocean, bathed in the lights from Seaview, reveling in the scent of the honeysuckle. She hadn't run into Adam that night and she wondered what had kept him.

Jenny's mood didn't improve much the next day. She was in a funk, trying to find someone who may have been connected with the dead man.

"Give it some time," Betty Sue Morse said sagely as she twirled strands of peach and white wool over her knitting needles. "You are thinking too hard."

"We are missing something obvious, Betty Sue," Jenny groaned. "But what is it?"

She pulled out the torn piece of paper from her bag and stared at it. It was a faded photograph, probably taken some time ago.

"Why didn't I think of that?" Jenny said suddenly, sitting up straight. "This is not a digital print. This looks like an old photo."

"Show me that," Heather said,

extending her hand toward Jenny.

She peered at the photo for a while.

"I don't know if this means anything," she said uncertainly, "but this man looks a bit different from the picture Star drew."

"Let me see," Star said. "I know what it is," she said, her face settling in a knowing expression. "The picture I drew shows an older man."

"Does that matter?" Jenny asked.

"It means you are right about this photo, Jenny," Star told her. "The man is much younger in this photo. So this must be old."

"Now why was the man carrying around an old photo of himself?" Betty Sue said, pausing in mid-stitch.

She put her knitting on the table and held out her hand. Star passed the picture to her.

Betty Sue looked at the photo carefully and tapped her finger excitedly.

"Of course this is old," she said. "Don't you see?"

She handed the photo to Petunia.

"Tell me what you see here."

Petunia looked bewildered. "It's just a picture of a man, Betty Sue. What are you going on about? Just get to the point."

"Don't you see that Ferris wheel in the distance?" Betty Sue asked. "This photo was taken right here, in Pelican Cove."

"How can you be sure?" Star asked, looking uncertain.

"Remember that year we had a Ferris wheel for the Summer Fest? Look at that picture closely, Star. I am sure this was taken right here, on our boardwalk."

"The festival you mention was almost ten years ago," Petunia said. "So this man was in town ten years ago too?"

"We just have to find out who was here at that time," Jenny said.

"Don't be so hasty, dear," Betty Sue said. "Most people in Pelican Cove have been here for generations. You're one of the few who just got here."

"The Newburys were here ten years ago," Star said, counting on her fingers. "Jimmy was here and so was I."

"Is there someone who wasn't here ten years ago?" Jenny asked. "We can strike them off as a suspect."

"You are the only one, Jenny," Heather said.

"I wasn't here," Molly said, pulling her head out of her book.

She had been quiet all this time.

"Neither were you, Heather. We were both living in the city at that time."

"You're wrong," Heather said. "I spent two weeks here in the summer that year. I was home for the summer festival. I remember riding that Ferris wheel with Chris."

"You were going out with Chris ten years ago too?" Jenny asked with a knowing smile.

"They have been together since they were knee high," Betty Sue said proudly. "They need to take the plunge and move ahead before the Grim Reaper comes for me."

"You're not going anywhere yet, Grandma," Heather said, hugging her grandmother.

Jenny tried to hide her impatience. She spotted a mop of red hair and wondered what the mailman was doing on the boardwalk. Kevin came into view, carrying his bag.

"Playing hooky, young man?" Betty Sue called out imperiously.

Kevin saluted them as he ran up the steps of the café.

"Howdy, ya'll. It's a fine spring day."

"Isn't it too cold for shorts?" Heather asked, trying not to stare at Kevin's bare acne covered legs.

"High of 75 today," he said. "I can't wait to start wearing my summer uniform."

"What can I get you, dear?" Petunia asked. "Muffin and coffee to go?"

"I'm on my lunch break," Kevin told them. "I think I am going to sit here and have a bite to eat."

"Have you tried Jenny's strawberry chicken sandwich yet?" Heather asked him. "It's delicious!"

"Here's your photo, Jenny," Heather said, handing it over. "I guess we've hit a wall again."

"What's that?" Kevin asked with interest.

"It's a photo of the dead man," Heather told him.

"Can I have a look?" he asked.

"Does he look familiar?" Jenny asked eagerly. "We figured out that he was here in town ten years ago. You might have come across him somewhere."

Kevin took the photo from Heather's hand.

"This was taken right here, on our boardwalk," he nodded.

Betty Sue looked around triumphantly with a 'told you so' look in her eyes.

"Never seen this guy before," Kevin said, giving the photo back to Jenny. "And I've been here all my life. I bet I would have seen him sometime."

"Strangers are easy to spot in Pelican Cove," Heather nodded.

"What a waste of time," Molly said, rolling her eyes. "I'm heading back to work."

"Have you noticed anything different about Molly?" Heather asked after she left. "She hardly participates in any discussion. Wonder what's eating her."

"That's it," Jenny said. "We need a girl's night."

"Movie, wine and pizza," Heather nodded. "I'm all for it."

"Wait till you taste my pear and prosciutto pizza," Jenny said eagerly.

"You're not cooking," Heather said, shaking her head. "We'll order a pie from Mama Rosa's. It's the best pizza in town."

"I can vouch for that," Kevin said, wolfing down his sandwich.

He waved goodbye to them after a while and left. Betty Sue and Heather headed back to the inn and Jenny went back to the kitchen. She was trying out a new lemon cake recipe that afternoon.

Petunia was sitting at the kitchen table with a frown on her face.

"Something doesn't add up," she

said to Jenny. "I am thinking back to the year of the summer festival, the year we had that Ferris wheel."

"What about it, Petunia?"

"Something's nagging me about it but I can't remember what."

"Is it important?" Jenny asked.

"I don't know," Petunia said, shaking her head. "But it's like an itch that won't go away."

"Stop thinking about it," Jenny consoled as she added the dry ingredients for her cake to a sieve. "It will come to you."

Jenny frosted some cupcakes and put them in the glass case out front. The café door opened and Adam Hopkins came in. He was leaning heavily on his cane and Jenny wondered if he was in more pain than usual.

"What can I get you?" she asked with a smile.

"How about that cupcake?" he winced. "And some coffee."

"You got it," Jenny said, adding cream and sugar to his coffee. "You know, I can run this over to the police station if we are not too busy. You just have to call us and place an order."

"You think I can't walk here on my own?" Adam growled.

"I didn't say that!" Jenny shot

back. "You're in a nice mood."

Petunia had heard the whole exchange. She rushed to explain.

"You know we deliver food in the season, Sheriff," she said primly. "We'll have more help once the kids line up for a job."

"I'm sorry," he said, sounding anything but.

"We just found out something about that man," Jenny said. "But I don't think I want to talk to you in this mood."

"Stop acting like a child, Jenny," Adam snapped. "If you have any information pertaining to a crime, you are obligated to report it to the police."

Jenny didn't like Adam's tone but she realized he was right. She leaned forward and spoke under her breath.

"He was here ten years ago."

"Who?" Adam asked, taking a big sip of his coffee.

Jenny pulled the picture out of her bag and showed it to Adam.

"That's the Ferris wheel from the summer festival," Adam said immediately. "The twins threw up all over my shirt after they rode on it."

"Do you not see the man in the picture?" Jenny asked, rolling her eyes.

"Where did you get this?" Adam asked urgently. "It belongs in evidence."

"It fell out of Jimmy Parson's wallet," Jenny said grimly. "Do you remember I told you about it? You weren't too interested."

"You didn't say anything about this picture, Jenny," Adam said, snatching it out of her hand. "How many people have touched this?"

"All of us," Jenny said reluctantly.

"You have been tampering with evidence. I thought you knew better than that."

"Don't lose sight of the bigger picture, Adam," Jenny shot back. "What was this man doing in Pelican Cove ten years ago?"

Chapter 17

Jenny's cranky mood persisted for a few days. Even Star and Petunia were afraid to talk to her.

"We are coming over tonight," Heather told her during their break one morning. "Pull out your favorite DVDs and get ready for some girl time."

"I saw a recipe for a homemade face mask," Molly said eagerly. "It's made with avocadoes and turmeric."

"We'll have a spa night!" Heather exclaimed. "You need to put your feet up and relax, Jenny."

Jenny finally cracked a smile.

"I have a foot spa I have never used...it has jets and everything. And a basket of foot care products my son Nick got me for Christmas."

"Why don't you come over to the inn, Star?" Betty Sue asked. "We can have our own soiree away from the kids."

Big plans were made and all the ladies went around with smiles on their faces. The night was declared a success.

Jenny had a spring in her step as she walked to the Boardwalk Café the next morning. She admired her freshly painted nails and grinned from ear to ear. The girls had given each other foot

massages and the avocado face
mask had worked wonders. The
girls had devoured a large 20 inch
pizza from Mama Rosa's and
Jenny had admitted it was the
best pizza she had tasted in a
while.

"We need to finalize our menu for
the Spring Fest," Petunia said as
she started the first pot of coffee.
"We will need to order in the
supplies and start prepping."

"Chicken salad sandwiches,
orange strawberry cupcakes and
bow tie pasta salad," Jenny
declared. "What do you think?"

"Isn't that a lot?" Petunia asked.

"The salads can be made the day

before, so can the frosting," Jenny said confidently. "Don't worry, I can handle it. My aunt will offer to help."

"Star and I will both be on hand," Petunia nodded. "You'll have some time to enjoy yourself with your beau, don't worry."

"I have a beau?" Jenny asked, raising her eyebrows. "How do I not know that?"

Petunia just laughed and shook her head. Jenny forgot all about it as the first customer of the day came in.

"Good morning, Captain Charlie," Jenny said brightly. "Your usual?"

"Hello ladies," Captain Charlie

smiled. "Good day to you too."

He thanked Jenny for his coffee.

"You need to get out on the water, young lady. Take a kayak out one day."

Jenny shuddered and smiled. She was terrified of being on a boat. She knew she would have to reveal her secret sometime soon. Heather had already asked her to go kayaking with her a couple of times. Molly kept talking about taking a boat out and going bird watching in the season.

"When do I have time for that?" she joked. "Petunia keeps me chained to this kitchen."

They chatted easily for a while

and Captain Charlie waved goodbye.

Jenny baked two batches of muffins and poured coffee for what seemed like hours until Betty Sue and Heather arrived for their mid-morning break.

"Take that apron off, Jenny, and sit down," Petunia ordered.

"Just as soon as I fill this order," Jenny promised.

She went outside a few minutes later and sat down next to Heather.

"Lady out there is having an early lunch," she panted. "She ordered the special."

Betty Sue didn't hide her curiosity as she looked around for this woman.

"Looks like a tourist alright," she remarked.

"She's been here before," Jenny told them after taking a sip of her coffee.

She had skipped breakfast due to the morning rush. She gratefully bit into a muffin and spoke between bites.

"Finish eating first, girl," Betty Sue ordered. "You are spraying crumbs all over the place."

Jenny swallowed a giant bite and took another sip of coffee.

"She's come to the café before," Jenny said again. "She noticed our menu has changed."

"Is she visiting someone in town?" Heather asked curiously.

"Maybe she's shopping for something," Petunia suggested.

The town of Pelican Cove had a small antique store that was well known in the region. People came there from far away, looking for some particular piece of jewelry or furniture.

"I gather it's the opposite," Jenny said in a hushed voice, leaning toward the women.

She felt like a voyeur although she hadn't been eavesdropping on purpose.

"I heard her talking on the phone. She is here to sell some family heirloom."

"There are only two possible places she is visiting then," Betty Sue declared. "The antique store or Ada Newbury."

"You think she knows the Newburys?" Jenny asked immediately.

She picked up her cup of coffee and gave the woman a speculative look. The woman was wearing a designer suit that cost four figures. Jenny recognized it from the catalog of a top departmental store. Even her makeup was expensive. The strand of pearls around her throat looked real.

"She could be going to the Country Club," Heather observed. "She is certainly dressed for it."

"Why would she eat here then?" Petunia asked.

"Maybe she's just killing time, waiting for an appointment or something," Jenny mused.

"You people have got to get a life," Molly complained. "Who cares who that woman is?"

"I do," Jenny said, standing up. "I am going to go ask her."

She started walking toward the

woman before anyone had a chance to react.

"Can I get you anything else?" she asked the woman.

"No, thank you," the woman said.

She didn't sound too forthcoming but Jenny forged ahead.

"Are you new in town? I've never seen you here before."

"It's been a while since I came to Pelican Cove," the woman admitted.

"Most people I meet have been here forever," Jenny said, purposely trying to sound over friendly. "It's great to see someone who's not from the shore."

"You moved here recently?" the woman asked politely.

Jenny nodded.

"Have you been to the antique store?" the woman asked. "They have quite a collection. Of course, young people these days aren't really interested in heirlooms."

"Are you a collector?" Jenny asked, feigning interest.

"Sort of," the woman said reluctantly. "I am here to sell something. It's been in my family for three generations."

"So you just take it to the store and offer it to them?" Jenny asked.

She was genuinely curious about this answer.

The woman seemed happy with the question. She gave Jenny a patronizing smile.

"Collectors are a tight bunch. We just put the word out when we want to sell a piece. Sometimes we hire an agent."

"Why would you pay someone a fat commission when you can directly talk to another collector?" Jenny asked.

"You're smart," the woman said approvingly. "But I have a limited circle of acquaintance. Agents have ties in other states, sometimes in other countries too."

"Wow!" Jenny exclaimed.

She was looking for a way to pull out of the conversation. The woman exclaimed suddenly and sat up with a jerk. She pointed toward the bulletin board that hung on the café wall.

"Why is that picture hanging there?" she asked in a shaky voice.

Jenny felt her heart speed up. She walked up to the board and put her finger on Star's drawing of John Smith.

"You mean this picture?" she asked, crossing her fingers behind

387

her back.

"Think of the devil..." the woman muttered. "I just talked about agents, right? This man is one of the sleaziest I have ever come across."

Jenny chose her words carefully.

"This man was in town recently. We are not sure why."

"He is exactly the kind of man the Newburys associate with. Ada Newbury must be up to something."

"You know Ada Newbury?" Jenny asked.

The woman had finally told her what she wanted to hear.

"She is the private collector I was talking about earlier," the woman said. "Looks like she's in the process of trading something too."

"You are sure Ada Newbury knows this man here?" Jenny asked again.

"Most antique collectors do," the woman nodded. "He's on the move all the time. I bet he didn't stay here long."

"He sure didn't," Jenny said cryptically.

The woman stood up and said goodbye to Jenny.

"Did you get that?" Jenny asked, rushing back to the table where her friends sat.

"Poor Grandpa Robert," Heather sighed.

"Julius tends to bend the rules, but he has never lied to me before," Betty Sue said.

"You didn't ask him about the man, Grandma," Heather reminded her.

"He definitely lied to the police," Petunia said. "I think the Newburys have gone too far this time. We tolerate Ada's high handed ways but murder? That's going a bit too far."

"Don't be silly, Petunia," Betty Sue snapped.

A sheen of perspiration had appeared on her upper lip.

"I am sure there is a simple explanation."

"Like what?" Heather cried. "Does this mean Grandpa Robert is in trouble?"

"Robert wasn't in town when the man died," Betty Sue reminded Heather. "Think before you speak, girl."

"Adam has to act on this," Jenny declared. "I am going to talk to him now."

"I'm coming with you," Heather said.

"We are taking Jason with us,"

Jenny said. "Adam can't brush him off that easily."

Jenny marched down the road to Jason Stone's office. Heather scurried behind her.

"Hello ladies!" Jason Stone greeted them with a pleasant smile. "What have you been up to now?"

Jenny gave him a brief account of her conversation with the woman in the café.

"I'm glad you didn't go off to confront the Newburys," he said. "Let's go and talk to Adam Hopkins first."

Adam was in the process of unscrewing a bottle of pain pills.

He frowned when he saw Jenny and popped a couple of pills in his mouth. He washed them down with a glass of water.

"What have you done now, Jenny?" he asked.

Jenny bristled with anger.

"I will let that slide for now," she thundered. "Wait till you hear what I have to say."

Adam leaned back and calmly heard them out.

"Thanks for bringing this to our attention."

"Is that all?" Jenny asked, her hands on her hips. "Why aren't you taking any action?"

"I am going to process the information you just provided and decide what to do next," Adam said, barely controlling his anger. "Not that I owe you any explanation whatsoever."

"Don't you see?" Jenny wailed. "I was right. The Newburys have been lying all along. What are they trying to hide?"

Adam turned to look at Jason.

"Take her away from here," he said. "Please!"

"Let's go, Jenny," Jason said, taking her arm.

Heather led the way out of the police station.

"He won't do anything," Jenny muttered. "He's going to sit in that chair and do nothing."

"Give him a break, Jenny," Jason urged. "You gave him some information two minutes ago. There is a process to be followed here. Adam is a good cop. He'll take the right action."

"Why do you think I am doing this?" Jenny asked miserably.

Her eyes filled with tears and Jason put an arm around her shoulders.

"I just want my aunt to be in the clear as soon as possible."

"I know that," Jason nodded. "But you can't rush these things. You will have to be patient, Jenny. You need to be strong. At least do it for Star."

"What happens now, Jason?" Heather asked, rubbing Jenny's back.

"The police will have to question the Newburys again. They might find some new information this time."

"Have we made any progress at all?" Jenny whimpered.

"You have come a long way, Jenny," Jason nodded. "You know the man was here in town, now and ten years ago. He visited the Newburys for some reason. You found out he is an antiques dealer. You are turning into a proper sleuth."

"You know how people in town spot a stranger from a mile away?" Heather asked. "I just can't get over why someone didn't see this guy."

Jenny remembered what Star had said to her before.

"Someone is lying to us."

Chapter 18

"Barb Norton is back," Betty Sue informed the group assembled at the Boardwalk Café one day. "She's already throwing her weight around."

"She just asked you about helping out at the Spring Fest, Grandma," Heather laughed.

"Exactly," Betty Sue bobbed her head. "Everything is already planned. All the duties have been assigned. What does she want now?"

"You are mad because she came back a few days later than usual," Heather said knowingly.

Betty Sue Morse smirked and

carried on with her knitting.

"Wait a minute," Jenny asked, sitting down next to her.

She had heard part of the exchange.

"Who is this woman?"

Petunia's chins wobbled as she took a deep breath.

"Barb Norton has a finger in every pie."

"She likes to participate in all the town events," Heather elaborated.

"You mean she tries to control everything," Petunia said. "She's going to stir the pot now that she is here."

"I don't remember meeting this woman," Jenny said lightly. "But she sounds harmless."

"She spends the winter in Florida with her daughter," Star explained. "She was already gone when you got here. She'll have a bunch of questions for you, honey. You'll see."

"I have nothing to hide," Jenny said grimly.

Jenny knew how small town gossip worked. When she first came to Pelican Cove, her separation had been too recent. She had stumbled through all the questions people threw at her, feeling awkward and shameful. But she was in a much better place now. She was ready for any inquisition.

"Barb's not that bad," Heather told her. "She's never been one of us though."

"She's not a Magnolia, you mean…"

Jenny had grown close to the group of women who met at the Boardwalk Café. None of them could get through their day without sharing a cup of coffee with each other. Star had suggested they name themselves. Plenty of names had been considered and discarded until Heather suggested 'magnolias'. She openly admitted it was inspired by her favorite movie.

Everyone had approved and the group had wholeheartedly christened themselves.

"So she won't be joining us for our mid-morning coffee breaks?" Jenny asked with a smile.

"Oh no!" Molly spoke up.

Jenny shrugged. Apparently there was something about this woman that rubbed her friends the wrong way.

"Yooo hoooo..." a cheery voice called out.

A short, well rounded woman came up the café steps from the boardwalk. Betty Sue rolled her eyes and put on a fake smile.

"Hello girls, how are you?" the woman said, peering closely at everyone's face. "You look like you got a few more wrinkles over the winter, Betty Sue," she said. "And who might you be?"

The woman was staring directly at Jenny with a question on her face.

"This is my niece, Barb," Star said proudly. "She lives in Pelican Cove now."

"Jenny King," Jenny said offering her hand. "Pleased to meet you, Madam."

"Oh, call me Barb like everyone else," Barb squealed. "Moved here from the city, did you? Well, well...what brings you here, young lady?"

"Let the girl breathe, Barb!" Betty Sue roared. "Sit down."

Barb Norton sat down next to Heather. She looked around the table with a gleam in her eye.

"So? Tell me...what have you been up to all winter?"

"Nothing much, Barb," Petunia said dully.

The women around the table mumbled and seconded her.

"I heard about the dead man, of course," Barb said in a hushed voice.

She looked at Star.

"You poor thing...I hear they arrested you. What have you done?"

"So much for keeping secrets..." Star muttered under her breath.

"Star is innocent," Jenny said firmly. "We are trying to prove that."

"Of course she is," Barb Norton agreed. "What have you done so far? Maybe I can help."

"How about some coffee, Barb?" Petunia asked. "And wait till you try our Jenny's cupcakes."

Barb Norton got distracted for a while. She gave them a detailed account of the time she had spent with her daughter. Every little thing she had done over the winter was revisited in detail. Betty Sue looked like a martyr as she focused on her knitting while listening to the woman.

"Have you painted the café recently?" Barb asked, standing up to look around. "It was long overdue, Petunia. A fresh coat of paint will attract more customers."

"We had an incident," Petunia responded meekly.

Barb Norton had moved on to the bulletin board. She read every little flyer out loud and gave her opinion on it.

"You can rest assured about the

Spring Fest," she declared to everyone around her. "I can take on some duties now that I'm here."

"All the jobs have already been assigned," Betty Sue called out from her table. "You know we finish that by mid February, Barb."

"Nonsense!" Barb dismissed her. "I am sure someone will be happy with a lighter load."

Jenny wondered if Barb would notice the picture of John Smith that was still up on the board. Barb jabbed her finger at the photo just then.

"This face is so familiar," she said

with a faraway look in her eyes. "Who is this?"

"That's the man," Jenny told her. "The one who died here in Pelican Cove."

"I've seen him before," Barb said, nodding her head. "I just don't remember when."

"Was it recently?" Jenny asked, trying not to sound eager.

"How can it be recent?" Petunia argued. "Barb has been gone for three months."

"All I can tell you is that I know this face," Barb repeated. "I never forget a face, you know. It will come to me."

"Show her the photo, Jenny," Star said. "She might remember that one."

"Didn't Adam take that from you?" Heather asked.

"He did," Jenny nodded, "but I already had a copy."

She pulled the photo with the Ferris wheel from her pocket and handed it to Barb.

"That's the summer festival here in town," Barb said immediately. "I was in charge of the photo committee that year. Maybe this guy appears in some other photos? I will have to look them up."

Jenny felt a surge of hope rise

within her.

"Oh please...can you do it at your earliest? It will help us figure out who the guy is."

"Don't worry, dear," Barb assured her. "I'll look into it."

Barb Norton left after she finished her coffee and cake. She had a lot of catching up to do in town.

"Barb is a meticulous record keeper," Betty Sue said graciously. "If there's anything to be found, she will find it."

"What did I tell you?" Petunia declared. "She's already riling things up."

"This is for a good cause," Jenny

reminded her.

"Wait till she makes us change our menu for the Spring Fest," Petunia muttered, getting back to the kitchen.

Jenny stepped out for her walk later that night, eager to run into Adam and Tank. She hadn't met Adam since she talked to him at the police station.

"His leg must be bothering him," Star said when Jenny got back earlier than usual.

"Huh?"

"Adam," Star said knowingly. "Why don't you go visit him tomorrow?"

"I have no interest in being insulted," Jenny said.

Her grouchy mood persisted the next morning. She poured coffee and served the customers without exchanging a single smile with anyone.

"You need a day off," Captain Charlie told her.

Betty Sue Morse thundered into the Boardwalk Café at 10 AM, Heather following close behind.

"Where is your car?" she asked Jenny.

"Grandma's run out of wool," Heather said, looking harassed.

It was the first time Jenny had

seen Betty Sue without her knitting needles.

"Are we going on a wool run?" she asked sullenly.

"We are going to visit the Newburys," Betty Sue informed her. "Get your car and start driving."

Heather piled into the back seat and the three of them set off for the Newbury estate.

"I am tired of the suspense," Betty Sue said as they climbed the road that led up to the Newbury mansion. "I want to settle this once and for all."

"Are you planning to confront Ada Newbury?" Jenny asked.

413

"Darn right," Betty Sue barked. "It's high time she came clean."

"We haven't called ahead," Heather said timidly. "She doesn't like people who turn up without an appointment, Grandma."

"I am going to meet my husband," Betty Sue said stoutly. "I don't need an appointment for that."

A maid showed them into the parlor.

"Tell Ada Betty Sue Morse is here."

The maid scurried away without a word.

Robert Newbury came into the

room and sat down in front of Betty Sue.

"This is a nice surprise," he said, smiling at Heather. "What brings you here?"

"I need to talk to Ada," Betty Sue began. "You better stay here, Robert. You need to listen to this too."

Ada Newbury came in a couple of minutes later. She was dressed to go out.

"Betty Sue? Heather! I was about to leave for my spa appointment. You would have known that if you had called ahead."

She paused meaningfully, as if waiting for an apology.

"Sit down, Ada," Betty Sue ordered. "You're not going anywhere until you talk to me."

Ada Newbury turned red and opened her mouth to object. Betty Sue beat her to it.

"Tell me what you did to that poor man. Tell me now."

Ada collapsed on a couch and cracked her knuckles. She seemed speechless for a change.

"What is all this, Betty Sue?" Robert asked his wife.

"We know you lied to us about not knowing that man," Betty Sue said, pointing a finger at Ada. "I want to know why."

"You have no right to question me," Ada said haughtily. "The police have already been here. We told them whatever they needed to know."

Jenny decided to step in.

"Mrs. Newbury, we are trying to find out as much as we can about that man. Your staff has confirmed he was here. Another woman from out of town told us you knew him well."

"This is none of your business, Miss King."

"I wish it wasn't," Jenny sighed. "But both my aunt and I are involved in this. Please, Mrs. Newbury, we need your help."

"What have you got to hide, Ada?" Betty Sue probed. "Why don't you come clean?"

Julius Newbury entered the room and sat down next to his wife. He took her hand in his and gave her a nod.

"This is kind of personal," Julius started.

"You can trust Betty Sue," Robert interrupted. "She's family."

Julius Newbury looked at Jenny.

"I'm not going to malign you, Mr. Newbury. I just want to get some information about that dead man."

Julius Newbury continued.

"John was a dealer in antiques. He acted like an agent or liaison."

"We learned that recently," Jenny admitted.

"We had something to sell," Julius coughed. "A very valuable heirloom, in fact."

"Something from the 'Bella, I bet," Betty Sue muttered.

"Anyhoo," Julius continued. "I put the word out. John was here on behalf of another collector."

"Is that when you shared a drink?" Jenny asked.

"He was here for dinner one evening," Julius confirmed.

"Do you remember what day it was?" Jenny asked.

"It was two days before the Spring Gala," Ada Newbury said. "I have it written down in my appointment book."

"How did your meeting go?" Jenny asked.

"Let's say it was favorable," Julius said. "We agreed on some terms and I was going to ship the object to the concerned party. I paid John my share of the commission."

"Did you have any disagreements?"

"Not at all," Julius said calmly. "It was a normal business meeting."

"Did he mention how long he was going to be in town?"

"He said he would stick around for a day or two."

"Did he say why?"

"I didn't ask," Julius shrugged. "Is that important?"

"He was alive for at least a day after he met you," Jenny mused. "Something happened to him during that day."

"Did you invite him to that party?" Betty Sue asked.

Ada's disdain was clearly written on her face.

"You know I am particular about

who I invite to my parties, Betty Sue."

"Then why was he here on your beach?" Heather asked.

The Newburys didn't have an answer for that.

"I noticed you called him John," Jenny said to Julius. "Was John Smith his real name?"

"John Smith?" Julius said sharply. "We knew him as John Mendoza."

Chapter 19

Jenny wasn't sure if their visit to the Newbury mansion had been productive.

"At least we know why they met that man," Heather said. "And we know his real name."

"We can't be sure of that," Jenny said glumly. "Maybe he had a string of aliases."

Jason Stone came to the Boardwalk Café bright and early the next day.

"What are you doing this evening?" he asked. "How about driving up to Chincoteague for dinner?"

"I could use a break," Jenny admitted.

She looked at Jason and bit her lower lip.

"It's not a date," he said, reading her mind. "It's just dinner."

"Will you pick me up?" Jenny asked him.

"See you at six," he said, waving goodbye. "It will take us an hour to get there."

Betty Sue arrived for coffee with Heather in tow. Heather was clutching a bag overflowing with bright yellow yarn.

"We just got a big shipment," she told Jenny, glancing at the bag.

"We have yarn in every possible color, enough to last Grandma for months."

Star joined them a few minutes later. She was wearing a paint splattered smock with two pockets at the front. A couple of paint brushes peeped out of one pocket.

"Do you always go around town like that?" Jenny asked her aunt.

Star nodded.

"I have a deadline. I need to finish a commission by tomorrow. I'm just here to grab a quick coffee."

"Would you notice if one of those brushes fell out?" Jenny asked her aunt.

Star shrugged.

"I guess. I will notice it's missing."

"I bet that's what happened," Jenny told her aunt. "You must have dropped a brush somewhere and forgot about it."

"But I don't remember going anywhere near that beach," Star argued. "Why would anyone pick up a paintbrush anyway?"

"We need to come up with a plausible reason," Jenny told her.

"Why do people do anything?" Star asked, quirking an eyebrow.

Jenny slapped the lid on a large paper cup full of coffee and handed it to her aunt. She added a bag with a warm muffin.

"I won't be home for dinner tonight."

"Has Adam finally asked you out?" Star asked with a smile.

Jenny's face hardened.

"I haven't talked to Adam in a while. I'm going out with Jason."

"Potato, Po-tah-to…" Star said as she waved goodbye to her friends.

"So you have a hot date tonight, huh?" Heather asked Jenny when she went back to their usual

427

table.

"It's just dinner," she repeated. "I'm not dating anyone."

"What's wrong with Jason?" Molly asked. "He's handsome and successful. And he's smart too. You could do worse than him."

"Jason's cool," Jenny agreed. "But my divorce isn't final yet, you know. And I'm not mentally there."

"Anything else?" Heather asked.

"Jason's a lawyer," Jenny said, rubbing the charms in her necklace. "Have you thought about that?"

"So what?" Molly and Heather

chorused.

"Hello! I was married to a lawyer for twenty years, and look how that turned out."

"Every person is different, dear," Betty Sue said, looking up from her knitting.

"Jason's a good boy," Petunia added. "And he's never been married."

"He's older than me, right?" Jenny mused, taking a sip of her coffee. "Someone should have snatched him up long ago."

"Maybe he never found the right girl," Heather sighed.

"You never went out with him?"

Jenny asked Heather.

"Jason's a lot older than me," Heather explained. "His sister was my babysitter."

"He's perfect for you, though, Jenny," Molly said with a grin. "So where are you going on this non-date?"

The girls teased Jenny mercilessly until they all burst out laughing. Jenny held up a hand, holding her side with the other. She had a stitch in her side from laughing too much.

"Enough! Let's talk about something else."

Jenny looked at Betty Sue. She was remembering what she had

said to the Newburys.

"What did you mean when you said something came from the 'bella'?"

"She meant the Isabella," Heather explained. "It was a steamship that went down in the shoals near the island."

"You know the story, don't you, Jenny?" Petunia asked.

"I have heard bits and pieces," Jenny said uncertainly. "But what does it have to do with the Newburys?"

"That's how the Newburys got rich," Molly said.

"Huh?"

431

"The Isabella sunk in the shoals around the island in 1876," Betty Sue started, putting her needles back in her bag. "Folks from the island tried to save them but there were only 17 survivors. The Isabella went down in the ocean. The survivors settled on the island. People dived on the wreck for years. They found little bits and pieces but nothing big."

Jenny's mouth was hanging open as she listened to this tale.

"Then we had the great storm of 1962," Heather continued. "Half the island sank at that time. The Morse family lost a large portion of their land."

"That's when Pelican Cove was

formed, wasn't it?" Jenny asked.

"The wreck of the Isabella shifted during the storm," Heather said in a hushed voice. "The Newburys dove on the wreck and salvaged a lot of things at that time."

"Why didn't anyone else dive on the wreck?" Jenny asked.

"Most people were fighting for their life," Betty Sue explained. "Houses were washed away. People were holed up in whatever shelter they could find. They were busy saving themselves or their neighbors."

"Everyone except the Newburys," Heather said. "They were seen going out to the wreck in a boat."

"It was foolhardy," Betty Sue snarled. "Robert's older brother was in that boat. He was swept away. They never found him."

"But they found treasure!" Heather added.

"How do you know for sure?" Jenny asked.

"The Newburys became rich overnight," Betty Sue said with a faraway look in her eyes. "They bought a huge tract of land from my Daddy and built their estate."

"And that's how the Newburys became the richest family in Pelican Cove," Heather finished.

"Do people hold a grudge against them for taking the treasure?"

Jenny asked.

"The survivors do I guess," Heather shrugged. "It came from their ship, after all."

"Why don't you ask Adam about it sometime?" Molly said with relish.

"Where did your family come from?" Jenny asked her.

"We came here from neighboring towns," Molly explained. "They were washed away during the Great Storm of 1962. Both my parents were young kids when their families sought shelter in Pelican Cove."

"What about your ancestors?" Heather asked.

"They were early settlers on the neighboring islands," Molly said, "just like the Stones and the Newburys and the other Pioneers."

"So most of your ancestors were British? Is that why the locals here speak with a different accent?"

"Until the bridge was built in the 70s, the only way to get here was by boat," Betty Sue explained. "The islanders were kind of isolated and they developed their own dialect."

Molly stood up to leave.

"I'm glad you are talking about something other than that

wretched man, Jenny. You've got a bee in your bonnet about him."

"No I don't," Jenny said in a hurt tone. "I am trying to protect my aunt. You would do the same thing in my place."

"Chris was talking to Ethan yesterday," Heather butted in. "The police are beginning to think it was someone from out of town."

"Who's Ethan?" Jenny asked.

"Adam's brother?" Heather sighed. "The guy who runs that fish shack at the other end of Main Street?"

"It kind of makes sense," Molly said. "We established that he wasn't from here. So the person harming him must also be from out of town."

"That doesn't make sense at all," Jenny argued. "Let's assume he wasn't from Pelican Cove. But he was connected to people here. He met the Newburys and he was going to meet someone else. We just need to know who that person was."

"Even if he knew someone else here," Heather considered, "what possible motive could anyone have to kill him?"

"That's the big question, isn't it?" Jenny sighed. "We won't know until we find this other person."

"If the police believe the killer came from out of town, they will have to exonerate Star," Molly pointed out. "You should be happy with that theory."

"I'm not saying it's impossible," Jenny explained. "But some things don't add up."

"Why would an outsider trash the café?" Petunia spoke up for the first time. "They wouldn't even know what's going on in town."

Kevin the mailman came up the café steps. He greeted them with his customary salute and handed over some mail to Petunia.

"Howdy ladies?"

"How are you, Kevin?" Petunia

asked. "Are you staying here for lunch?"

"I think I will just get a coffee to go," Kevin said. "Got a whole bunch of mail to deliver today."

"Would you know if there was someone new in town?" Jenny asked Kevin as she poured his coffee.

"I would know if they got any mail delivered," he said, scratching his head. "Why do you ask?"

"Don't worry about it," Jenny said. "Just a thought I had."

The group broke up after that and Jenny got busy with the lunch rush. She hurried home after work, thinking about what she was going to wear. She ran into Adam just outside the Boardwalk Café.

"Tank and I were going for a walk. Want to join us?"

Jenny hadn't forgiven Adam for his churlish behavior.

"Not tonight," she shook her head. "I'm going out to dinner."

Adam's jaw tightened and he gave her a nod. He pulled at Tank's leash and walked away before she had a chance to hug the dog.

Jenny's mind was consumed by Adam as she walked home. Had he wanted to talk about something?

She pulled out a pale green dress from her closet and paired it with a denim jacket. She hoped it wasn't too casual for the place Jason was taking her to.

"You look beautiful," Jason said as he sipped cold beer from a plastic cup.

He had taken her to a crab shack situated right on the water. They ordered a huge platter of fried seafood. Jenny dipped a hush puppy in tartar sauce and tried not to blush.

"We're not on a date, remember?"

"When do you think you might lift this dating embargo?" Jason asked, biting into a crunchy coconut shrimp.

"How was your day?" Jenny asked with a laugh, neatly side stepping his question.

"A lawyer's life can be pretty monotonous," Jason told her. "I spend most of my time reading boring law journals."

"Don't you have a paralegal?"

"I don't need one," Jason said honestly.

"Do you miss the city?"

"Sometimes," he said honestly. "But I don't miss the eighty hour work weeks and the rat race. I am ready to settle down and take it easy."

"Are you thinking of having kids?" Jenny asked him.

"At my age?" Jason laughed. "Chances are slim to none, unless I adopt someone or start fostering."

"My son Nick is the best thing that came out of my marriage," Jenny admitted honestly.

"You know what? This sounds very much like a first date conversation."

"Let's talk about something else then."

"How is Star?" Jason asked. "We should have some good news for her soon."

"She's fine...busy working on her commissions. Have you talked to Adam recently?" Jenny asked.

"I have," Jason affirmed. "The police are pursuing a different theory. They are almost convinced someone from out of town is responsible."

"Heather mentioned that," Jenny told Jason. "But I'm not so sure."

"Neither am I," Jason agreed with her. "And do you know why? I keep coming back to the attack on the café."

"Me too," Jenny said, dunking a couple of fries in ketchup. "I have a feeling it's someone around us, someone we know very well."

Chapter 20

Jenny enjoyed her evening out with Jason Stone. But she couldn't let go of a premonition. She was beginning to think someone was spying on her and she had no idea why.

"Tell me I am being silly, Heather," she pleaded the next morning.

The Magnolias were enjoying their usual coffee break.

"You are being silly," Heather parroted. "What's all this, Jenny? You seem nervous."

"I have this feeling that someone's watching me," she said, sounding illogical even to herself.

"You mean like an intuition?" Heather asked.

"Maybe," Jenny said thoughtfully.

"Are you psychic?" Molly asked her. "Do you dream about something before it happens?"

Jenny rolled her eyes.

"I don't believe in that kind of stuff."

"You're jittery," Betty Sue told her. "Too much coffee can do that to you."

"I never drank so much coffee before coming here," Jenny agreed. "That's it. I'm switching

447

to herbal tea."

"Are you worried about the Spring Fest?" Petunia asked her. "You are going to be a big success, my dear. And we will all be on hand to help you."

"It's not that," Jenny shook her hand.

"How about another movie night?" Molly asked. "I can host this time."

"That sounds like a good idea," Heather approved.

"How was your dinner date?" Molly asked her. "Don't think you can distract us, Jenny. We want to know every little detail."

"Jason ordered a big platter of fried food and I ate like a glutton. Really, you should have seen me stuff my face."

"So you feel comfortable around him," Heather said. "That's a good start."

Jenny wondered if she was a bit too much at ease with Jason. She was beginning to like him a lot but her heart didn't beat wildly when she thought of him.

"Yooo-hooo..." a shrill voice called out.

Barb Norton waved at them from the boardwalk, looking excited. She was clutching a shoebox to her bosom. She huffed up the café steps and came to their table. She slammed the box down and collapsed in an empty chair.

"It's all there," she panted.

"Take a deep breath, Barb," Betty Sue ordered. "Calm down."

Barb gulped several mouthfuls of air and her chest stopped heaving. Her cheeks were pink and her eyes shone wildly.

"What did I tell you, Betty Sue? I never forget a face."

"Did you find the guy in the photo?" Jenny asked, jumping up.

"I did," Barb said triumphantly. "Wait till you hear what I have to say."

Molly stood up and started leaving.

"Where are you going, missy?" Barb thundered. "Sit down!"

"I need to get back to work, Barb. I don't have all day."

"You can't run far," Barb said cryptically. "Will you sit down now?"

Molly's face had turned green. She sat down in her chair. Jenny noticed her balled fists and wondered what that was about.

"Tell us about the guy, Barb," Jenny prompted.

"I was in charge of the festival photos ten years ago," Barb started. "We had a booth set up where people could pose for photos and ask for prints. We also took photos of everyone as they came in, just in case they wanted a copy later. That's how we raise money, see?"

Jenny tried to curb her impatience.

"I kept a copy of every photo. They were in a box in my attic. It took me a while to locate the box."

She pointed at the shoe box giving them an idea of what it contained.

"So he came to the summer festival then?" Heather asked in a hushed voice.

"He sure did," Barb sneered. "And he wasn't alone."

A collective gasp went around the assembled group. Jenny noticed Molly wasn't looking too good.

"That photo you have there," Barb pointed. "That is just half of a picture. Here's the actual one."

She pulled out a faded photograph from the shoebox and thrust it in Jenny's hand. Jenny stared at the picture and the face of John Smith or John Mendoza. He was smiling into the camera with his arm around a young girl. She was holding a giant tub of popcorn and laughing into the camera. Something about that picture struck Jenny but she wanted to be sure. She handed over the photo to Heather.

Heather took one look at the picture and sprang up.

"You lied to us!" she screamed. "Why did you do that, Molly?"

"That man was Molly's beau!" Barb informed them. "She was working in the city that summer but she came back home for the summer festival."

All eyes turned toward Molly. She was shaking like a leaf.

"Is that true?" Betty Sue asked gently.

"Of course it's true," Barb interrupted. "She introduced him to me, told me she wanted a copy of that picture."

"Let the girl speak, Barb," Petunia urged.

Molly burst into tears. She stood up and rushed down the stairs of the café and ran across the boardwalk to the beach.

"Let her go," Jenny said.

She was feeling overwhelmed.

"She's been lying to us this whole time," Heather voiced her thoughts. "We thought she was one of us."

"She could have saved us a lot of

trouble," Betty Sue agreed. "But she must have a reason for all this."

"What reason could there be?" Jenny argued, her hands on her hips. "She knows the agony Star and I have been through. She's been sitting here calmly day after day, watching us suffer."

"I agree with Jenny," Heather said stoutly.

Kevin came up the stairs and saluted them.

"Something wrong?" he asked as he saw all the frowning faces.

No one answered him.

He handed over some mail to

Petunia and looked around.

"What's up with Molly?" he asked.

He was pointing somewhere near the water. Molly stood knee deep in the water with her back to them.

"She's cooling off," Barb chuckled.

No one noticed when the mailman turned around and went away. Jenny was on the phone in the kitchen. She had decided to call Adam.

"What's wrong, Jenny?" Adam asked when he heard her voice.

"We have some new information about the murder," she told him. "Maybe you should come here."

457

She went outside and told the ladies. "The sheriff will be here soon."

Molly had turned around and come back up the café stairs. Her dress was wet at the hem and she was shivering. Petunia offered her a blanket and poured her a cup of fresh coffee.

"What were you thinking, going in the water like that?"

Adam Hopkins arrived and came out on the deck.

"What's going on, ladies?" he asked grimly.

Barb opened her mouth and told him about the old photo. He studied the photo and looked at

Molly.

"That's you alright, Molly," he said. "You want to tell us how you know this guy?"

"You can start by telling us his real name," Heather snapped. "Is it John Smith or John Mendoza?"

"You don't have to say anything here, Molly," Adam said. "You can come to the police station and give me a statement."

"I want them to hear this," Molly said.

She looked around at the assembled women.

"His name was John Mendoza," she started. "He was my

husband."

Another gasp went through the group.

"I divorced him before I came back to Pelican Cove."

"So I was right," Barb beamed. "You did introduce him to me."

"It was senior year of college," Molly nodded. "We had been dating for two years. I knew I wanted to spend the rest of my life with him. That's why I brought him here. I wanted to show off the town, introduce him to my parents."

"Why did you hide this from us?" Jenny asked. "You could have spared everyone a lot of trouble."

"She's right," Adam said. "You wasted police resources by withholding this information."

"So sue me," Molly said defiantly.

"You didn't spare a thought for my aunt, did you?" Jenny demanded. "You just watched us squirm."

"John was my past," Molly pleaded. "He was a part of the life I left behind."

"You must have been shocked when you saw the picture Star drew," Betty Sue said.

Molly said nothing.

"Maybe she didn't recognize him from the picture," Jenny said,

461

trying to cut her friend some slack.

"What about the picture Jenny found in that wallet?" Heather asked. "That's a photo of that man, right? You must have realized who he was then?"

"Did he know you lived here in Pelican Cove?" Petunia asked.

"Not exactly," Molly whispered. "We didn't part amicably."

"Why did you get a divorce?" Adam asked. "It's a matter of record so I will find it out eventually."

Tears rolled down Molly's eyes.

"We got married soon after we

graduated. I got a job in a big library in the city. John didn't have a permanent job. He just fixed deals for people and earned commission."

"He was an antiques dealer," Heather supplied. "We know that."

"Things were fine for the first couple of years. Then he started drinking. Other things followed..."

"Like what?" Heather asked, her mouth hanging open. "Did he hurt you, Molly?"

Molly gave a barely perceptible nod.

"I had a mentor, an older woman who was my boss. She helped me get a lawyer and file for divorce. I decided I was never going to lay eyes on him again."

"And then he turned up dead right here in town," Betty Sue prompted. "No wonder you didn't want to say anything."

Molly stared at the floor, refusing to look up.

"What else are you hiding from us, Molly?" Jenny asked. "You met him, didn't you?"

"Yes," Molly whispered.

"Was it at the party?" Heather asked.

"She wasn't invited there," Betty Sue said. "It must have been somewhere else."

Molly gulped and started talking again.

"John came to town looking for me. He wanted to talk to me."

"Stop right there, Molly," Adam said. "Be very careful about what you are going to say. You know you can hire a lawyer, right?"

"I haven't done anything wrong," Molly said shakily. "John came to my door and I turned him away. But he kept trying to talk to me."

"You hadn't talked to him at all in all these years?" Heather asked her.

Molly shook her head.

465

"I had no idea where he lived. The apartment we lived in was rented and we both moved out at the same time. I didn't have an address for him after that."

"What was so important after all these years?" Jenny asked her.

"He said he wanted to apologize," Molly said meekly.

"Did you believe him?" Petunia asked.

"It didn't make any difference to me," Molly sighed. "I stopped trusting that man long ago."

"What about the Newburys?" Betty Sue asked. "How do they figure in all this?"

"He said he was in town for a deal," Molly told them. "I suppose he just wanted to check on me, see where I lived."

"So he just wanted to say sorry?" Heather asked.

"He wanted me to forgive him. Said he had been sober for a while and was doing some kind of 12 step program. He pleaded for my forgiveness."

"Did you believe he had changed?" Barb Norton asked.

"Something came over me," Molly said. "I screamed at him and told him to go away."

"Atta girl!" Betty Sue smiled approvingly.

"You need to come with me, Molly," Adam Hopkins interrupted. "I need to take down your statement. And I have to ask you some questions."

Molly followed Adam out of the café. Everyone started talking at once.

"What did I tell you?" Jenny burst out. "I was right, wasn't I? She was right here all this time, watching us."

"Do you think she killed him?" Heather got to the point.

"You know her better than me, Heather."

"Stop talking nonsense, girls," Betty Sue ordered. "Molly

Henderson didn't kill anyone."

"Then who did?" Barb asked.

No one had an answer to that question.

Chapter 21

Jenny moved around in a daze all day. She had called Star at her gallery and told her about the whole Molly incident. Like Betty Sue Morse, Star also stood by Molly.

"I know her mother, you know," Star said. "I remember the day Molly was born. There's no way she had anything to do with this."

"I disagree," Jenny had said firmly. "Molly is involved one way or the other."

Petunia had reserved her opinion on the topic. She didn't want any of her friends to be implicated.

"The police are not going to tell us

much," she told Jenny. "Molly's the only one who can shed some light on what went down at the police station."

Jenny debated going to the library to meet Molly. She wasn't sure if Molly had been detained or if she was back at her desk at work. Molly answered that question by turning up at the café later that afternoon. Petunia and Jenny had just finished cleaning up and were prepping for the next day.

"Molly!" Jenny exclaimed as she saw her come up the steps of the Boardwalk Café.

Molly almost collapsed when Jenny took her by the arms. She was looking drained.

"Have you had any lunch, dear?" Petunia asked with concern. "Let me get you something to eat."

"Have you been with Adam all this time?" Jenny asked Molly.

Her protective nature had overcome any reservations she may have had about Molly.

"What for?" she cried.

"They had some questions," Molly said softly.

Her voice was barely audible and Jenny leaned closer to hear her better.

"You have been gone for hours."

"I called Betty Sue," Petunia said

grimly as she placed a plate loaded with potato chips and a chicken sandwich in front of Molly. "Start eating, young lady. And don't say a word until you have finished all that."

"Do you prefer iced tea or coffee?" Jenny asked, trying to be helpful.

Molly's eyes filled up as she took a bite.

"You know I'm innocent, don't you?" she pleaded.

"My aunt thinks so," Jenny said, unsure of her own opinion.

Petunia had put up the Closed sign and the café emptied soon after. Betty Sue and Heather rambled up, followed by Tootsie. Heather had her on a leash. Tootsie trotted up to Molly and nuzzled her.

Molly gave Tootsie a hug and cried softly.

"I thought you needed some comfort," Heather said. "How are you holding up, Molls?"

Star joined them a few minutes later. She patted Molly on the shoulder and gave her a hug.

"I know you had nothing to do with killing that man," she said curtly.

"The police say I have a strong motive," Molly explained.

"Having a motive isn't enough," Jenny said. "Did you have an opportunity to do this?"

"They say I don't have an alibi," Molly said.

"Did they ask where you were at a particular time?" Jenny wanted to know.

"They asked me where I was for a couple of days, the day of the party and a day before that."

"That's quite a wide window," Jenny observed.

"They asked me about those days too," Star nodded.

"You never told me that," Jenny said, surprised.

475

"It never came up," Star said with a shrug. "And I didn't think it was important. I never set eyes on that man in my life."

"You left John Mendoza a few years ago, didn't you?" Heather asked. "What motive could you have to kill him?"

Molly looked sad as she contemplated an answer.

"John hurt me. Really hurt me. I had to go to the emergency room a few times. There is a record of all my injuries."

"Did you tell them your husband was abusing you?" Jenny asked.

"At the time, I just said I had bumped into something. But it came up during the divorce. John wasn't ready to let me go. Then his lawyer came up with a lot of nasty stuff against me. That's when I finally reported him for physical and mental abuse."

"So it's all part of an official record then," Jenny summed up.

Molly nodded.

"The police think I was bearing a grudge against him, or I am scarred or something."

"Who would blame you if you were?" Betty Sue Morse said, stroking Tootsie.

Tootsie had climbed up in her lap and was dozing with one eye closed. She was staring at the

assembled group with the other.
The little poodle sensed
something was wrong.

"So what? You bashed his head or
something?" Jenny asked
incredulously. "If you had hit him
in a fit of anger, he would have
been dead right there at your
doorstep."

"That's exactly what I told them,"
Molly cried. "Why would I lure him
to a deserted beach and attack
him?"

"How big was he?" Jenny asked.
"Was he stronger than you?"

"He was about the same size and
build," Molly said.

"You need to get a lawyer, Molly,"

Jenny said decisively. "You need one whether you are guilty or innocent."

"Jason Stone is the only lawyer in town," Heather reminded them. "I don't think he can represent both Star and Molly at the same time."

"Not unless they drop the charges against Star," Jenny nodded. "I wonder if they will do that."

"Lawyers are expensive," Molly said. "I am not sure I can afford someone pricey from out of town."

"What are you going to do then, Molly?" Betty Sue Morse asked.

Molly turned toward Jenny with a question in her eyes.

"Can you help me, please?"

"I'm not on speaking terms with my husband," Jenny said, misunderstanding her. "And he's a different kind of lawyer."

"I need *your* help," Molly corrected her. "I want you to continue working on this, Jenny."

"I was just showing a photo around, Molly," Jenny protested. "I'm not a trained investigator."

"You can continue asking questions," Star said, "just like you did before."

"I can't promise any results," Jenny warned Molly.

"We know nothing about John

Mendoza's life," Heather spoke up. "Did he have any enemies?"

"I had no contact with him since I came to Pelican Cove," Molly reminded them. "He was a bit unscrupulous, but I think that was common in the business he was in."

"Could someone have followed him here to Pelican Cove?" Petunia asked as her chins wobbled in unison.

"That brings us back to the whole outsider theory," Jenny said. "How did anyone in town not see this person?"

"How long would it take to do the deed, turn around and drive out of town?" Betty Sue asked them. "That beach where they found him is almost deserted, remember?"

"There's one person who could have seen this stranger," Heather said.

"Jimmy Parsons?" Jenny asked. "I doubt he will admit it."

"Jimmy's a good guy," Star said. "He won't sit on something on purpose."

The group went back and forth, evaluating different scenarios and discarding them. Betty Sue finally stood up when Tootsie started pulling at her leash.

"I need to take Toots for a walk,"

she said. "I think we all need a break."

"Do you want me to come home with you, Molly?" Heather asked. "I can keep you company for some time."

"What about that Movie Night you girls were talking about?" Petunia asked. "I think tonight's as good a time as any for it."

Jenny felt torn inside. She needed some quiet time to herself so she could gather her thoughts. She also wanted to talk to Adam.

Molly solved her problem.

"I think I will turn in early tonight," Molly said. "I have a headache."

"Let's at least go to the Rusty Anchor for a while," Heather urged.

Molly hesitated. A glass of wine sounded good to her.

"I'm going to call Chris," Heather said, pulling her cell phone out of her bag. "He can meet us there."

Star agreed to go with them to the pub. Betty Sue walked off with Tootsie. The girls headed to the Rusty Anchor accompanied by Star.

Chris was already there when they went in. Eddie waved at them from the bar and pointed toward a table. He had reserved it for them. He came over with a glass of chilled white wine and placed it before Molly.

"This is that Chardonnay you like from our local winery," he told her.

He gave her a pat on the back.

"Don't worry, Molly. We are with you. I know you wouldn't harm a fly."

Molly nodded awkwardly and took a deep sip from her glass. The others kept the conversation going, trying to draw a smile out of Molly.

Jenny spotted a familiar red headed figure at the bar.

"Isn't it a bit too late for

delivering mail?" she muttered.

Heather looked up at the bar and spotted Kevin waving at her. She waved back.

"He's off duty, Jenny," she whispered.

Kevin came over holding a mug of beer.

"You guys celebrating something?" he asked with a smile.

"Sure," Chris said, slapping him on the back. "Why don't you join us?"

The group broke up soon after that. Chris and Heather insisted on accompanying Molly home.

Star and Jenny decided to collect a pizza for dinner on their way back home.

"I thought I was going to be bored in Pelican Cove," she told her aunt. "But I haven't had a single spare moment since I got here."

"It's not even summer yet," Star laughed. "Wait till the tourists get here."

They ran into Jason at Mama Rosa's. He was waiting for his own order.

"Have you heard the news?" Jenny asked him.

"I've been in the city all day for a case," he told them. "I'm just getting home."

"Want to join us for dinner?" Star asked. "We can bring you up to speed."

Jenny put in an order for a large veggie pizza and three salads. She figured two pizzas would be plenty for the three of them.

"Are you going to make me eat salad?" Jason teased.

Star set out knives and forks when they got home and popped open the salad boxes.

"What did I miss?" Jason asked, spearing a cherry tomato with his fork.

Jenny gave him a brief account of

the day's developments.

"This might be good news for you," Jason told Star. "I am talking to the sheriff first thing tomorrow morning."

"What is your take on all this?" Jenny asked as she took a big bite of her veggie pizza.

"I've known Molly since she was a kid," Jason said thoughtfully. "But it's hard to say. They say victims of abuse can be scarred for life. Who knows what kind of trauma Molly has faced. She might have panicked or just lashed out at him."

Jason didn't stay around long after dinner. Jenny forced herself to go for her walk. A new patch of rose bushes had bloomed at Seaview and Jenny leaned against a post, taking in their beauty. A pink climbing rose twined up a trellis and shimmered in the silvery moonlight. Another white rose bush covered the front wall of the mansion. Jenny felt Seaview was a bit too grand to be called a cottage.

A hairy body leapt over Jenny and she sat down in the sand with a thud.

"Tank! You naughty boy!" she laughed as Tank began licking her face all over.

Jenny kissed the burly Labrador and looked around for Adam.

Adam whistled softly and Tank bounded back to him. Leaning on his cane with one hand, Adam offered the other one to Jenny. She pulled herself up and dusted the sand off her clothes.

Jenny tried to curb the thrill she felt when she looked at Adam. She wanted to ask why he hadn't come to the beach for the past few days. Instead she said something completely different.

"Molly's innocent. I don't know why you are treating her like a suspect."

"And here we go again…" Adam said with a sigh.

Chapter 22

Adam Hopkins refused to disclose any information about the case.

"I've told you before, Jenny," he barked at her one evening on the beach. "Stop interfering and let us do our job."

"Molly's going through hell," she told him. "You have known her longer than me. Don't you care about her at all?"

"I can't take sides," Adam sighed. "I'm just doing my job."

Ada Newbury started a campaign to get Molly fired from her job.

"She's talking to the board members," Molly told them one

morning over coffee. "She is saying I am a bad influence on the kids coming to the library."

"How so?" Jenny asked with her hands on her hips.

"I don't know," Molly cried. "Maybe because I was married to John?"

"Does she know how he treated you?" Heather burst out. "You are not the villain of the story."

"Ada's just throwing her weight around," Betty Sue told them. "That's what she does best."

"I can't lose my job," Molly said tearfully. "There aren't any other jobs in Pelican Cove. Who's going to hire me if I get fired for bad character?"

"Don't worry," Betty Sue consoled Molly.

She was a member of the library board.

"I will talk to the others and make sure they know the whole story."

"Have you found any more clues, Jenny?" Molly asked her.

"I'm hitting a wall," Jenny admitted. "John Mendoza's photo is still up there on our bulletin board. Nobody has come forward with any more information."

"How about putting an ad in the county paper?" Petunia suggested. "It's circulated in some of the neighboring towns too."

"We can try posting online again," Heather added.

"Let's do that," Jenny agreed. "We'll try both the methods. We need all the help we can get at this point."

"Has Star remembered anything about her paintbrush?" Betty Sue asked.

Star had another deadline and wasn't with them that morning.

Jenny shook her head. "She still maintains she could have dropped it anywhere. She's in some kind of zone when she paints. She's totally unaware of what's going on around her."

The ads in the paper didn't yield anything. Jenny couldn't shake the feeling that Molly was connected to the crime in some manner. She decided to probe further. She sat down with Molly one evening and began questioning her.

"Have you done anything different in the last few weeks, Molly?" she asked. "We don't know what we are looking for exactly. So don't spare any detail."

Molly thought for a while.

"I have a set routine. I go to work around 7:30 AM. I come here for my break. I eat lunch at my desk most days. I go home after work."

"Have you joined any classes? Visited a new store?"

Jenny felt she was just grasping at straws.

"Have you made any new friends, Molly?"

Molly shook her head after every question.

"You are sure you had no contact with John?" Jenny pressed. "Did he call you, Molly? Maybe you talked to him on the phone."

"Trust me," Molly said. "I haven't spared a thought for John in years. We parted on really bad terms. There was no way I would

497

talk to him."

"Have you noticed anything odd around you?"

"You're the only new person in my life, Jenny," Molly said with a smile.

Then her face clouded over.

"I almost forgot. Something weird did happen. I thought I was being forgetful."

"What do you mean?" Jenny asked, sitting up in her chair.

"I forgot to carry my lunch one day, so I went home to get a bite to eat."

"And?"

"Something seemed odd. I hadn't cleared up that morning, see? My tea cup was on the left side table. I always put it on the right."

"You couldn't have mixed it up?"

Molly shook her head in denial.

"I always hold the cup in my right hand. I put the cup on the table to the right. The table on the left holds my books. I always read at least two or three books at a time."

"Where were the books?" Jenny asked.

Molly closed her eyes and sat forward with a jerk.

"They weren't there! They were

on the mantel."

"You are sure you didn't put them there?"

"That's what I thought at that time," Molly said.

"You could have been mistaken, I suppose," Jenny mused, scratching her chin. "This is flimsy at best. And there's no one else to confirm it."

"Wait a minute," Molly said, jumping to her feet.

She rubbed her hands and began pacing around Jenny.

"How could I forget this?" she muttered.

"Forget what?" Jenny asked, her eyes shining with hope.

"My door was slightly ajar one day," Molly told her. "I thought I must have forgotten to shut it."

"Don't you lock your door when you go out?" Jenny asked in a shocked voice.

Molly gave her a look.

"This is Pelican Cove, Jenny. We don't lock doors here." She corrected herself. "The front door is locked from inside. Hardly anyone comes through that door. The back door is unlocked. I just shut it when I go out."

"Had things been moved around again?" Jenny asked.

"No," Molly said. "Not that I noticed. But the faucet in the kitchen sink was on. It was almost as if I had forgotten to shut it off before leaving."

"Had you?" Jenny asked.

"I've never done that before," Molly said.

"Did you tell anyone about this?"

"I forgot about it myself," Molly admitted. "If this was summer, I would have figured one of the kids came in for a drink of water."

"Do you keep any valuables at home?" Jenny asked Molly.

"I don't own any," Molly said simply.

"Is anything missing from your house, Molly?"

"I haven't really checked."

"We are going to check now," Jenny said. "Do you want to call Heather to help us?"

The three girls gathered at Molly's house and turned it upside down. Thankfully for them, Molly was a neat freak. She also didn't have a lot of stuff. All her winter clothes neatly hung in the closet. The rest were packed away in vacuum sealed bags. The five pairs of shoes she owned were lined up on a small shoe rack.

"So?" Heather asked after they had gone through every room. "Is anything missing?"

"I don't think so," Molly said. "I counted my books too. I don't know the name of every title but all 549 of them are here."

Jenny suddenly narrowed her eyes.

"What about any men in your life, Molly?" she asked. "Are you seeing someone?"

Molly's sad smile was answer enough.

"I have stayed away from relationships since my marriage broke up. I just wasn't ready."

"But has anyone asked you out?" Heather asked.

"You know most of the eligible single men in town," Molly said with a laugh. "And none of them are interested in me."

"That's because you never go out and have fun," Heather pouted. "You need to get out more. I'm going to ask Chris to set you up with one of his buddies. Then we can double date."

Jenny noticed a blush creeping up Molly's ears. She wondered what Heather had said to spark that.

"Let's call it quits for now," Jenny said with a sigh. "I'm starving."

"I'm craving something hot and deep fried," Heather nodded. "Why don't we head over to

505

Ethan's?"

"That's Adam's brother, right?" Jenny asked.

"You've never been to Ethan's Crab Shack?" Heather asked incredulously. "We are going there right now."

Jenny tried to hide her surprise when she came face to face with Ethan.

"You're Adam's twin!" she exclaimed.

"Guilty as charged," he grinned.

Ethan Hopkins looked exactly like his brother, yet he was completely different. Jenny realized she would never mistake him for Adam. The same pair of blue eyes looked back at her but they had a twinkle in them that was missing in Adam's eyes. Ethan was a big man, easily towering over six feet but he had a paunch that was absent in his brother. Probably comes from all that fried food, Jenny thought to herself.

Ethan waved them over to an empty table. The rustic wooden table was almost on the water. Jenny allowed herself to relax as she gazed at the vibrant orange sky juxtaposed against the salt marshes.

Heather ordered a pound each of shrimp, oysters and fish. Ethan came over with a large platter of fried goodies.

"This will get you started," he said.

The platter held heaps of fried mozzarella sticks, hand cut fries and hush puppies. Heather picked up a canister of Old Bay seasoning and sprinkled it over everything.

"The Old Bay makes everything better," she told Jenny.

Tiny bowls of ketchup and tartar sauce were placed in the center of the platter. The girls had chosen beer to go with their food.

Jenny took a long sip of her beer and chewed on a fried mozzarella stick.

"Save room for the seafood," Molly warned her.

"I'm stumped," Jenny declared, her mouth hanging open as Ethan came over with the fish. He placed a big bowl of coleslaw on the table. Breaded jumbo shrimp, beer battered fish and steamed crab followed.

"All set, ladies?" Ethan asked.

"Seen Adam today?" Heather asked cheekily, giving Jenny a wink.

Jenny couldn't control the blush that stole over her.

"He should be here by now," Ethan nodded. "The twins are here for the weekend and we are having a family dinner."

"Did you hear that?" Heather asked, nudging Jenny.

"Adam can't stop talking about you," Ethan told Jenny. "And those walks on the beach are helping him a lot."

"They don't make his leg hurt?" Jenny asked.

"It hurts anyway," Ethan said. "Exercise helps loosen up the stiff muscles."

"Walks on the beach?" Heather asked as soon as Ethan went back to the counter. "What are you hiding from us, Jenny?"

Jenny heard a familiar voice and

spied Captain Charlie talking to Ethan. He came over to greet the girls.

"Brought the catch in myself," he beamed. "It doesn't get any fresher than that."

The girls chatted with him for a while.

"I think Captain Charlie's got a thing for you too," Molly teased Jenny after he left.

"Don't be silly," Jenny said. "He's pushing sixty."

The girls demolished all the food, laughing and joking over silly things. Molly was looking better than she had in days.

Adam came in with the twins just as they were leaving.

"Hi Jenny," the girls chorused. "Want to have a drink with us?"

"I don't want to intrude on your family gathering," she said uncertainly.

Then her hand flew up to her mouth as she tried to stifle a burp.

"I'm ready to burst."

"We'll see you at the Spring Fest," the girls said. "We can't wait to try your strawberry cake. Dad can't stop raving about it."

The girls giggled all the way back through town.

Jenny and Petunia were busy the next two days, preparing for the Spring Fest. It was the first town festival Jenny would be attending and she couldn't curb her excitement.

"Why don't you go shopping for a nice dress?" Star suggested.

She looked around at Molly and Heather. "You should all go."

"I ordered a dress online," Heather nodded. "It should be here today."

"I'm not trying to impress anyone," Molly protested.

"Do it for yourself, sweetie," Star said, patting her back.

Jenny remembered what she had planned to do. It was nothing more than a hunch. She walked to the Pelican Cove High School later that day, armed with some questions. She went to the library and asked to look at old yearbooks.

"You didn't go to school here, did ya?" the old, faded lady at the school said.

"No, I didn't. But my friends Heather and Molly did. I am working on a surprise for them."

"What do you need their yearbooks for?" the woman grumbled. "They are stored up there." She pointed toward some shelves near the ceiling. "I will have to ask one of the kids to climb up a ladder and get them down for you."

"Can we do that now?" Jenny asked.

"No," the woman said flatly. "Come back next week. I need some advanced notice about these things."

Jenny bumped into someone on her way out and waved when she recognized Kevin.

"What are you going to find in those yearbooks?" Star asked when Jenny grumbled about them later.

"I'm shooting in the dark," Jenny admitted. "Maybe the past will give us the answers we are looking for."

Chapter 23

The day of the Spring Fest arrived soon enough. Jenny was hopping with excitement. She had been working overtime to get everything ready for the festival. The Boardwalk Café was going to have a booth and all her friends had promised to take turns dishing up Jenny's delicious food so she could have some free time to enjoy the festival herself.

Her phone rang as she was frosting the last of the cupcakes. It was her son Nick.

"Big day, Mom!" he said. "I know you'll do great."

"I wish you were here, Nicky,"

she whined, calling him by his childhood name. "I've met some girls who are about your age."

"Why didn't you say that first?" he joked.

Nick hung up after a while, leaving Jenny with a wistful feeling. She was beginning to like Pelican Cove but she wasn't too happy about being situated so far from her son.

"Let's start loading the van," Petunia said.

She had solicited the help of some high school kids to help them load everything. The fairgrounds where the festival was being held were barely a mile away from the

Boardwalk Café.

"We couldn't have just walked these over?" she asked Petunia.

"It gets old after the third or fourth trip," Petunia said. "Trust me on that."

The whole town of Pelican Cove seemed to have gathered for the festival. Betty Sue Morse cut the ribbon, holding Tootsie in her arms and implored everyone to have fun.

The goodies from the Boardwalk Café were flying off the shelves.

"I hope you saved one of those cupcakes for me," a voice drawled.

Jenny looked up into the stormy blue eyes of Adam Hopkins.

"Aren't you tired of eating these?" she teased.

"Why don't you show her around, Adam?" Petunia said. "It's time she took a break and let her hair down."

"I thought I had dibs on showing you around," Jason Stone said, appearing next to Jenny.

He put his arm through hers and whisked her away, making her laugh at something silly. She mouthed 'sorry' to Adam Hopkins who shrugged and began walking away.

"Adam's going to be mad at you,

Jason."

"He's mad at someone most of the time," Jason laughed. "Forget about him."

Jenny felt a twinge of discomfort at the thought of disappointing Adam. Then she forgot all about it. They ran into Chris and Heather at the cotton candy booth. Heather was leaning into Chris, her face lit up in smiles. Jenny figured things must be going well with them.

"Have you seen Molly?" she asked, tearing off a big piece of the pink floss.

She popped it into her mouth and let it melt on her tongue.

"Let's get some real food," Jason said, pointing to a barbecue truck. "Those ribs are calling my name."

"Will you go get us some?" Jenny asked. "I need to sit down for a while."

Jason nodded cheerfully and strode toward the food stalls. Jenny was sure he would get more than just ribs. She found it was easy being around Jason. She didn't feel like she had to watch every word she said.

Jenny wandered around looking for a place to sit. She spotted a couple of plastic chairs stacked over one another behind a tent. Almost every table around her was taken. Jenny thought she had lucked out with the empty chairs. She walked around the tent to get them. Everything around her went black the next instant. She saw stars and felt herself sinking into an abyss.

A beeping sound woke Jenny up. She had a massive headache. Her son Nick's face swam in front of her eyes.

"Nicky," she croaked. "Where am I?"

"That was some stunt you pulled, Mom," her son smiled. "If I had known how badly you wanted me here..."

Jenny shifted her gaze and spotted a host of familiar faces.

Star, Molly, Heather, Petunia and Betty Sue were all crowded around her. She felt another hand in hers and realized Jason was sitting by her bed holding her hand. Jenny's heart sped up as she sensed another presence. Adam leaned on his stick in the doorway, standing away from the others.

"Clear the room, please," he ordered gruffly. "I need to talk to Jenny."

Nicky and Star both kissed her and filed out of the room. Jason didn't budge from his position.

"I'm staying right here," he informed Adam. "Someone has to keep an eye on her."

"I'm not here to hurt her, Jason," Adam said in an incensed voice. "Anything but."

His voice went down an octave as he spoke to Jenny.

"Do you think you can answer a few questions?"

"I have some questions of my own," Jenny muttered. "What am I doing here, for starters?"

"You were attacked," Adam told her. "Someone knocked you out and left you behind a tent."

"How did I get here?"

"We spent an hour looking for you," Jason said in an anguished voice. "Tootsie found you behind a tent. You were unconscious. The paramedics revived you and brought you here."

"What time is it?" Jenny asked.

"Eight in the evening," Adam said grimly. "Do you remember what hit you?"

"Are you sure I didn't just trip over something and fall down?" she asked.

"There was a Post-It note taped to your forehead, warning you to stay away," Jason told her.

"I want to know what you have been doing for the past few days, Jenny," Adam interrupted. "Someone out there is feeling threatened by your actions."

Jenny told Adam about Molly. Adam's eyebrows shot up when he heard about the queer happenings in Molly's house.

"She should have reported that," he sighed. "Who else have you talked to?"

"I don't think the school librarian is going to bash your head in," Adam said after he heard about her visit to the high school. "Did anyone else hear you talking to her?"

Jenny shook her head.

"The library was empty, as far as I remember."

"Think harder, Jenny," Adam urged. "This is important."

"Do the police suspect anyone of John Mendoza's murder?" Jenny asked.

She didn't expect Adam to give her an answer.

"We don't have any suspects at this time," Adam admitted. "We are beginning to think it was some unknown person from out of town. He was the type of person plenty of folk had a grudge against."

"That's a stupid theory," Jason lashed out. "The attack on Jenny proves the killer is someone we know. He or she has been a step ahead of us all along."

"What about Jimmy Parsons?"

Jenny asked. "He might have done it in a drunken daze and forgotten all about it."

"Jimmy has an alibi," Adam said. "He was helping Captain Charlie unload the catch. He was hanging out at Ethan's after that."

Jenny winced as a piercing pain ripped through her head. She rubbed her forehead and asked Jason for a drink of water.

"She needs to rest," Jason told Adam.

Adam turned to leave.

"Molly," Jenny whispered.

She wasn't sure if Adam heard her.

Star stayed in Jenny's room all night, sleeping by her bed in a chair. She had convinced Nick, Jason and all the girls to go home.

Molly was back the next morning, lugging a stack of yearbooks.

"These are the books you wanted," she told Jenny. "Old Mrs. Birch at the high school called me about them."

Jenny didn't have to voice her question. Molly held up a hand and explained.

"She said you mentioned us when you wanted to see the yearbooks. She called me when you didn't turn up to get them. Small town, you see. Everyone knows everyone."

Jenny smiled weakly. She had completely forgotten what she was going to look for in the yearbooks.

"I can't believe how dorky I was in high school," Molly laughed as she helped Jenny sit up in bed. "Don't laugh too hard, okay?"

Jenny looked at the six feet tall scrawny figure of Molly Henderson. Had she always worn those soda bottle glasses, Jenny wondered. The yearbooks would tell her that.

Nick came in to meet Jenny. He was followed by the Magnolias.

Heather handed her a bunch of pink and white roses. Jenny looked surprised as she breathed in a familiar fragrance.

"I picked this bouquet from Seaview's garden," Heather told her. "I know how much you love the place."

"When can I go home?" Jenny asked Star. "I confess I'm enjoying all the attention. But I'd rather enjoy it from the comfort of home."

"Just a day more," Star told her. "They want to keep you under observation."

Jenny looked at her son. "You never told me how you got here so fast, Nicky."

Nick and Star looked at each other and started laughing.

"I was in Norfolk when I called you that morning," Nick told her. "I was going to surprise you at the Spring Fest. But you trumped me, Mom."

"I'm glad you are here," Jenny said tearfully, "but I'm sorry I can't show you around."

"Adam's twins are taking care of that," Betty Sue told her. "Your boy's going to be breaking hearts up and down the coast, Jenny."

"Don't cry, Mom," Nick said, handing her a tissue. "You're going to be fine."

"She's just emotional," Star said. "Why don't we all go get some coffee? We'll let her rest a bit."

Jenny closed her eyes and dozed off for a while. Nick was sitting in the chair next to her bed when she woke up. He was listening to some music on his headphones. Jenny's eyes fell upon the yearbooks Molly had placed by her bed. She started flipping through them. She spotted Heather and Chris and another red headed boy who looked familiar. He was standing next to Molly and another girl in a lot of the pictures. Judging by the photos, Chris had been the quarterback of the school team and quite a jock. Heather wore braces but Molly didn't have glasses.

The door opened and Molly walked in with another bunch of flowers.

"I forgot to bring these earlier," she apologized. "Jason got them for you. I ran into him this morning. There's a card with them."

Jason had scrawled a brief note telling her he had to be in court.

Jenny thanked Molly for the flowers and the message.

"These are interesting," Jenny said, pointing to the yearbooks in her lap. "You didn't wear glasses in school?"

Molly blushed.

"I wore contacts," she admitted. "I wanted to look cool for my boyfriend, you know. I didn't want to be the girl with the Coke-bottle glasses."

"You were seeing someone in high school?" Jenny asked.

"You'll never guess who. I kind of dumped him when I went away to college. We just wanted different things from life."

"Who?" Jenny whispered hoarsely.

"Kevin! The mailman. Can you imagine?" Molly laughed. "There's a reason why people shouldn't get hitched in high school."

"Kevin," Jenny repeated. "Is he that red haired kid in your yearbook?"

"Sure is," Molly bobbed her head. "He took the first job he got after graduation. Been a mailman ever since."

Jenny's heart began beating wildly. There was a knock on the door and Adam limped in. He wasn't looking too happy. He seemed relieved to see Molly.

"I'm glad I found you here, Molly," he said. "I was coming to you next."

"More questions for me?" Molly asked.

"Jenny told me about the stuff

you misplaced. I sent a few men to your block to make inquiries. We may have found something."

"I'm all ears," Molly said, sitting down.

"Are you up for this, Mom?" Nick asked.

He had taken off his headphones a while ago and was listening to what was going on.

"I'm okay!" Jenny assured everyone. "Get on with it, Adam."

"One of your neighbors sits in her sun room all day," Adam told them. "I guess she stares at the street and spies on people."

"You mean old Mrs. Daft?" Molly

snorted. "She's a voyeur alright."

"This voyeur may help us crack our case," Adam told them. "She has seen someone peering through your windows in the afternoon. This person goes in sometimes and spends some time in your house."

"But I'm at work all day," Molly said, shocked at this information.

"The woman, Mrs. Daft, wasn't sure of that. She thinks you might have an arrangement. She has seen you coming home for lunch sometimes."

"That's only if I forget to carry my lunch," Molly objected. "Is this woman sure I'm home when the man goes in?"

"She wasn't," Adam said. "She started noting down the days the man peeked in or went inside your house."

"Why would he do that?" Molly asked, sounding puzzled.

"Forget the why," Jenny cried. "Think of the who." She stared at Adam, trying to read his expression.

"Who is this man, Adam?"

Chapter 24

Adam was worried about Jenny. She was getting worked up.

"Calm down, Jenny," he said. "You too, Molly. At this time, we just have a description from Mrs. Daft. But I think it is enough to identify the person."

"Who is it?" Molly asked impatiently.

"It's the mailman," Adam told them.

"Kevin?" Molly and Jenny burst out together.

"The uniform and the red hair both point to only one person. We are bringing him in for questioning as we speak."

"Nothing was taken from my house," Molly said. "What's the crime here, Adam?"

"Trespassing at the least and murder at the most," Adam shot back.

"You think Kevin killed John?" Molly asked incredulously. "Why would he do that?"

"We are going to find that out," Adam told them. "Why don't you come with me, Molly?"

Nick's mouth was hanging open in shock.

"What have you been up to here, Mom?" he gushed. "I thought you were moving to a remote island where nothing interesting happened."

"So did I, son," Jenny said, pulling Nick into a hug.

Star and Petunia brought lunch from the Boardwalk Café.

"I made chicken noodle soup for you," Star said. "And Petunia made her special three cheese sandwich."

"Has anyone heard back from Molly?" Jenny asked, sipping the delicious thyme flavored soup. "I'm dying to know what's happening there."

Molly didn't come back until 4 PM. She looked drained.

"Have you had lunch?" Jenny asked with concern.

"Adam ordered some Chinese food for lunch," she said. "But I wasn't really hungry."

"Tell me what happened, Molls," Jenny urged. "Did he do it?"

"He did," Molly said, nodding her head. "He denied everything at first. Said Mrs. Daft must be mistaken. But he sang like a canary when he saw me."

Jenny would never have guessed what Molly told her next.

"He never stopped loving me," Molly said in wonder. "He never went out with any other woman. When I came back to Pelican Cove after my divorce, Kevin felt a surge of hope."

"Did he ever ask you out?"

Molly shook her head.

"He was giving me time to recover. He had finally decided to ask me out when he saw John arguing with me at my doorstep."

"Did he know John was your husband?"

"He did. He actually remembered his face from back when John had come here for that summer festival."

"Did he feel threatened?"

"No," Molly shook her head. "He

was sure I wouldn't go back to John."

"It's rare to have that kind of faith," Jenny mused. "Why would he think that?"

"Deep down, he believed I loved him too."

"What did you do to make him feel that, Molly?"

"Nothing," Molly said, shrugging her shoulders. "I hardly ever noticed him. I mean, I ran into him all the time on the street or at the café, but I didn't spare a thought for him."

"You must have talked to him though."

"I said Hello, Jenny, asked him how he was – just the usual polite talk you engage in with anyone you know."

"Did you go on a date with him? Share a cup of coffee or something?"

"Nothing like that," Molly said.

"Okay, go on."

"Kevin heard part of our conversation. He followed John to the beach. He waited until they got away from town and came to a deserted stretch. Then he confronted him and asked him to leave me alone."

"Was this the day of the party? Why didn't he run into any

picnickers?"

"This was earlier that morning, much before any of Ada's guests or the other people thronged the beach."

"John must have argued with him," Jenny said, considering how it had ended.

"They got into a fight. Kevin slugged him with a piece of wood he picked up. He felled John with a single blow."

"Was it an accident?"

"Kevin said he didn't mean to kill John. He just wanted him to stay away from me."

"What happened next? Did he just

walk away from there?"

"He knew John was dead," Molly told Jenny. "He must have known. He took John's wallet and took out his driver's license. He buried the wallet in the sand."

"Jimmy Parsons must have found it there!"

"Kevin had one of your aunt's brushes. He found it lying somewhere while delivering mail. He placed the brush in John's hand."

"What did Star ever do to him?" Jenny cried.

"He just wanted to confuse the police."

549

"Did Kevin think he would get away with this?"

"He was pretty confident," Molly said. "He was sure none of the people in town knew who John was. And then you stepped in and started looking into the whole thing."

"Did he deface the café?" Jenny asked angrily.

Molly sighed.

"Petunia chose that day to turn up early. He got away just in time."

"What about the attack on Jenny?" Star asked from the doorway.

Neither Jenny nor Molly had

noticed Star and Nick come in. Petunia, Heather and Betty Sue huddled behind them.

"Did you get any of that?" Jenny asked.

"We heard it all," Betty Sue said. "That Kevin! He was under our noses all the time, spying on us."

Heather shushed her grandma and looked at Molly.

"Did he really hurt Jenny?"

"He saw her at the high school, asking about yearbooks. He thought she would see our pictures and figure it all out."

"Now I remember Molly dated him in high school," Heather spoke up.

"We all thought they would get married after graduation."

"I always planned to go to college," Molly argued. "Marriage was the last thing on my mind."

"It was the first thing on his, apparently," Heather sniffed.

A nurse came in and shooed them all out.

Jenny found her eyelids drooping and she fell into a deep sleep.

Two days later, Jenny was back home with Star. She finally felt strong enough to go for a walk on the beach. The familiar scent of roses and honeysuckle perfumed the air around Star's cottage. The sky was ablaze in shades of pink and mauve. The weather was pleasant enough to go out without a sweater.

Jenny had received a fat envelope by courier that afternoon. Her divorce was final. Her lawyer had got her a big settlement. She got the house in the city and another vacation home they had in the mountains. Her husband wanted to continue living in their old home with his new family. He had offered her cash instead and she had accepted. She also had a fixed monthly payment coming to her for life. The judge had awarded her half of all remaining assets. Jenny's future was secure. Her whole life stretched before her and she had the means to live anywhere in the world. But

Pelican Cove had carved a special place in her heart.

She spotted a familiar yellow body bounding toward her across the sand. Opening her arms wide, she steeled herself for the impact.

"Tank! You darling! I have missed you so much."

Tank showed his affection by licking her all over her face.

Jenny's heart gave a leap and announced Adam's presence.

"Feeling better?" he asked her.

"That's what I get for interfering in police business."

"You did good, Jenny," Adam said

reluctantly. "He almost got away."

Jenny shuddered as she thought of Kevin and his smiling face. He had charmed them all with his salutes and his cheery greetings.

"He was there all along," she quivered. "He was one step ahead of us."

"Not anymore," Adam reminded her. "You are safe now, Jenny. You don't have to worry about anything."

"It will be a while before I stop looking over my shoulder," Jenny admitted.

She pulled a tennis ball out of her pocket and tossed it in the distance. Tank ran to fetch it.

"He was devious, wasn't he? He purposely planted that paintbrush on the dead body to frame Star. He was thinking ahead."

Adam cleared his throat.

"That wasn't the sole reason we suspected your aunt. Someone saw her on the beach the day before the Spring Gala. She didn't remember going there."

"Why didn't you tell me that before?"

"I couldn't. It was an ongoing investigation."

Jenny realized she had misjudged Adam.

"I miss my son," she told him. "It

was nice having him here for a while. He got along well with your twins."

Adam's face lit up in a smile. It completely transformed his face, making him look a bit like Ethan.

"They text each other all the time now," he told Jenny. "They are planning to spend some time here in the summer."

"Awesome!" Jenny said happily. "I'm so glad they hit it off."

"Some things are so easy when you are young," Adam said cryptically.

Jenny saw him wince in pain and slowed down.

"Do you want to take a break?" she asked.

Tank was walking beside them, his tail wagging vigorously.

"I'm fine," Adam snapped.

"Why do you come all the way to this beach?" Jenny asked him. "Is it because it's a smooth stretch without any rocks?"

"Something like that…" Adam said, looking away.

"Shall we turn back?" Jenny asked, stifling a yawn.

"Ethan is holding a barbecue at his place," Adam said in a rush. "Do you want to check it out?"

"You mean the Fool's Day BBQ?" Jenny asked. "I'm already going. Jason told me about it. Sounds like fun."

"You're going with Jason?" Adam mumbled.

"We are all going," Jenny said eagerly.

Adam nodded and stared at the horizon.

"So you are going to stay on in Pelican Cove?"

"This is my home now," Jenny told him. "Where else would I be?"

***

Did you enjoy this LARGE PRINT edition? Please write and let me know if you want to read the rest of my books in Large Print.

Thank you for reading this book. If you enjoyed this book, please consider leaving a brief review. Even a few words or a line or two will do.

As an indie author, I rely on reviews to spread the word about my book. Your assistance will be very helpful and greatly appreciated.

I would also really appreciate it if you tell your friends and family about the book. Word of mouth is an author's best friend, and it will be of immense help to me.

Many Thanks!

Author Leena Clover

http://leenaclover.com

Leenaclover@gmail.com

http://twitter.com/leenaclover

https://www.facebook.com/leenaclovercozymysterybooks

Other books by Leena Clover

Pelican Cove Cozy Mystery Series -

Cupcakes and Celebrities

Berries and Birthdays

Sprinkles and Skeletons

Waffles and Weekends

Muffins and Mobsters

Parfaits and Paramours

Truffles and Troubadours

Sundaes and Sinners

Dolphin Bay Cozy Mystery Series

Raspberry Chocolate Murder

Orange Thyme Death

Apple Caramel Mayhem

Meera Patel Cozy Mystery Series -

Gone with the Wings

A Pocket Full of Pie

For a Few Dumplings More

Back to the Fajitas

Christmas with the Franks

Join my Newsletter

Get access to exclusive bonus content, sneak peeks, giveaways and much more. Also get a chance to join my exclusive ARC group, the people who get first dibs on all my new books.

Sign up at the following link and join the fun.

Click here →
http://www.subscribepage.com/leenaclovernl

I love to hear from my readers, so please feel free to connect with me at any of the following places.

Website –
http://leenaclover.com

Twitter – https://twitter.com/leenaclover

Facebook – http://facebook.com/leenaclovercozymysterybooks

Instagram – http://instagram.com/leenaclover

Email – leenaclover@gmail.com

Printed in Poland
by Amazon Fulfillment
Poland Sp. z o.o., Wrocław

56076881R00334